D0065112

Also by Francesca Kay

An Equal Stillness

The Translation of the Bones

A Novel

Francesca Kay

SCRIBNER

New York London

Toronto Sydney New Delhi

SCRIBNER
A Division of Simon & Schuster, Inc.
1230 Avenue of the Americas
New York, NY 10020

Originally published in Great Britain in 2011 by Weidenfeld
& Nicolson, an imprint of The Orion Publishing Group Ltd.

First Scribner hardcover edition January 2012

SCRIBNER and design are registered trademarks of
The Gale Group, Inc., used under license by
Simon & Schuster, Inc., the publisher of this work.

For information about special discounts for
bulk purchases, please contact Simon & Schuster
Special Sales at 1-866-506-1949 or
business@simonandschuster.com.

The Simon & Schuster Speakers Bureau can bring
authors to your live event. For more information or
to book an event, contact the Simon & Schuster
Speakers Bureau at 1-866-248-3049 or visit
our website at www.simonspeakers.com.

Manufactured in the United States of America

10   9   8   7   6   5   4   3   2   1

ISBN 978-1-4516-3681-9
ISBN 978-1-4516-3683-3 (ebook)

To Teresa, and in memory of Bernard

Now faith is the substance of things hoped for, the evidence of things unseen.

—Hebrews 11:1

The Translation of the Bones

It's beyond belief what you find between the pews, Mrs. Armitage was saying. Coins and gloves you might expect, but socks and underwear? Hair clips, buttons, handkerchiefs, and now look at these, these peculiar white pills. She held out her hand to Father Diamond, who looked at it carefully and shook his head. Mrs. Armitage brushed the pills into the plastic rubbish sack beside her and went on: d'you know, the other day there was an old chap in here who was looking for his teeth? I said to him, I said I think you need a dentist not a church. But no, he swore he'd left them here and we had to have a good look round . . .

Excuse me, Father Diamond said. Behind him the sacristy door opened and Stella Morrison came out, her arms full of dying flowers. She stepped into a band of sunshine that streamed through the high windows of the south wall and for a moment she was wrapped in gold. Father Diamond turned and looked at her, the sunlight woven through her hair and spilling on the sheaf of fading roses and gloriosa lilies that she carried. She genuflected briefly in the direction of the altar and said: look, the last flowers we were allowed and now they're dead. She went on down the aisle to the main door. Excuse me, he said again to Mrs. Armitage, I can hear the minutes of the council meeting calling, I'd better love you and leave you, I'm afraid. Oh but, she said, but Father, I did want to have a word with you about the candle grease on that new surplice, and she put her hand firmly on the sleeve of his soutane.

Mary-Margaret O'Reilly watched Father Diamond's disappearing back less wistfully than usual as he followed Mrs. Armitage into the sacristy. She had been waiting for this moment, for this quiet, empty church. Now was the perfect chance. Mrs. Armitage had finished with her sweeping and her polishing; the great mop she used, stiff and black with floor wax, was back in the cupboard in the porch. If Mary-Margaret could get the job done now, and quickly, she'd have things shipshape before Father D put up the purple shrouds. She'd hate to think he'd see the dirt that she had noticed when she was gouging candle wax out of the pricket stands.

The problem was she could not find the ladder. She had thought there was one in the cupboard. But a chair would have to do instead. She took one from the back of the church and carried it through to the Chapel of the Holy Souls. There, with a silent prayer of apology for offense unwittingly caused, she stepped out of her shoes, climbed on the chair and from it onto the altar. She would change the white cloth later. Now she was face-to-face with Him, their eyes were level.

It had been difficult to choose the right materials for the task. Flash was far too harsh and so was Mr. Muscle. Fairy liquid, maybe? No, she felt this called for something special and, having rejected Boots as ordinary, she decided on the Body Shop at the top of the King's Road. The mingled scents she found there befuddled her a little, and she wasn't sure what to say to the powdery lady who bore down on her with an offer of help and a sample of glow enhancer. But she stood her ground and found the shelves of brightly colored bottles arrayed under the heading BODY CARE.

There was such a range to choose from. Papaya, clementine and starflower; fig, mango, passion fruit and melon. He had cursed a fig tree, hadn't He? Passion fruit perhaps? That might be suitable. The wounds, the crown of thorns. But when she sniffed it she felt the scent was far too womanly; He would want something cleaner and more masculine. Essence of pine? Would that make Him think of home, of wood, the shavings from His father's workbench, fat blond curls of clean-cut timber, or the wood of His own cross? Hang on though, was that not made of olive? Of course. Now she saw it was entirely obvious. Body wash with extract of virgin olive. Olives must have been his bread and meat.

The containers came in two sizes; she chose the smaller. It was still expensive. She also bought a pot of olive body cream.

The air was still and heavy in the church; sunlight, which had glistened briefly, gone. Mary-Margaret had already soaked the sponge she'd been carrying all week in Holy Water. It was a real sponge, the organic kind, not the nasty blue or pink thing you would use to clean the bath. It too had been expensive but she knew that it was necessary and, like the olive oil, would make Him feel at home. That is, if the sponge came from the Red Sea as she thought all sponges did. Or was it from the Dead? Well, in any case. The sponge absorbed all the water in the stoup, leaving nothing for the visiting faithful, but that could not be helped. Father Diamond would refill it later, she was sure. Now, standing on the altar, she took the wet sponge from the sandwich bag in which she had temporarily stowed it, and transferred it to the little plastic bowl she had also been carrying in her shopping bag. She unscrewed the cap of the body wash and poured half of it onto the sponge. It was not easy to do this while balancing on the altar, trying to hold the bowl at the same time. She could have done with an extra hand.

She began with His poor, wounded head, so cruelly pierced with thorns. With infinite tenderness she stroked the frothing sponge across His matted hair, around the rim of the torturers' crown. His eyelids drooping with tiredness and pain, His nose, His cheekbones taut beneath the skin, His beautiful, suffering mouth. The length of each arm straining from the crossbeam; His hands most horribly pinioned to the wood. She had packed a J-cloth, already moistened, this time with mineral water, and a dry one too for the rinse and final polish. As she wiped away the grime that had settled on His palms, going carefully around the rusty nails, she imagined that she soaked away His pain and sorrow as a mother would. His mother, or her own. She saw a child perching on the white rim of a bathtub, small grazed hands held out to gentle adult ones, trusting them to wash away the hurt with cooling water, make it better with a kiss. This picture was not a memory of her own. She pressed her lips briefly to His hands.

She could hardly bring herself to touch the deep gash in His side. His ribs protruded so painfully through His flesh, it was as if He had starved to death upon the cross. Years ago the nuns had told her how a person died from crucifixion. In effect He suffocated, exhausted from heaving Himself up against the agony of the nails for every breath. No one should be able to contemplate His passion and stay dry-eyed, the nuns had said, and Mary-Margaret could not; not then, nor ever. Now, dabbing at the dirt that overlaid His emaciated chest, her eyes were overflowing.

At the cloth that covered His loins she paused. The sculpted folds fell gracefully; after she had washed them they glowed white again, as they must have done when new. She wiped the froth away and dried them. To clean His legs and feet she knelt down on the altar. Those crossed feet pierced through by a single cruel nail. She remembered Mary of Magdala drying them with her hair; long it must have been, and flowing; long enough for her to wrap it round His feet as she bent over them, for she would not have dared to raise them to her head. Mary-Margaret's hair was too short to be used as anything other than a mop.

What was nard, she wondered, the pure nard that Mary of Magdala had got into such trouble for, when she poured it over His dear head? Probably it was very like the cream in the green pot she now took from her shoulder bag— buttery and thick and costly. Rich with the scent of herbs. Not simply olive, she imagined, but the others in the Gospels: hyssop, aloe, myrrh.

On the narrow altar she struggled back onto her feet, feeling a little giddy. The tiled floor beneath her suddenly seemed a long way down. By accident she knocked the plastic bowl, spilling the remaining foam. She tore the seal off the green pot, opened it and scooped up some of the ointment with her fingers. With endless love and reverence she stroked His sacred head. There were scabs where the thorns were rammed right through the scalp. She felt warmth against her hand. When she lifted it from His wounds she saw that it was red.

That evening Stella Morrison did not tell her husband Rufus that she had found poor Mary-Margaret unconscious on the floor of a side chapel. It would have been so easy to miss her, lying there in the dim light; it must have been some extra sense that prompted Stella to look right on her way back to the sacristy. That and the faint trace of an unfamiliar smell, something sickly and synthetic overriding the eternal ghost of incense that breathed out of the church walls. She had only gone back for her forgotten car keys, but she had looked, and she had seen a body sprawled there on its side, one arm flung out, a halo of blood around its head. She had thought that it was dead.

Poor Mary-Margaret, with her elasticated denim skirt scrumpled up about her thighs, her flesh-colored knee-high socks. Stella had checked that she was breathing, and called an ambulance. She had remembered that she must not move the body, in case of spinal damage. She had run to fetch Mrs. Armitage, who, thank goodness, was still in the sacristy with Father Diamond. Together they watched over Mary-Margaret, the three of them kneeling round her, until some kindly paramedics came and carried her away. Stella had to leave then because she was already late for her meeting with the volunteers of the Citizens Advice Bureau. Mrs. Armitage had cleaned up the mess all on her own. Well, Mary-Margaret was already two sandwiches short of a full picnic, Mrs. Armitage had said. Lord knows what she'll be like now.

Stella did not tell Rufus anything of this because she knew he would not be interested. And he would not have time in any case to listen. He didn't get back from the House that night until eleven o'clock, and he was hungry. Stella was hungry too, but Rufus expected her to wait for him; he disliked eating on his own. She cooked fillets of trout with tarragon and crushed potatoes, and she listened while Rufus talked about the crisis over MPs' expense claims. It would be an outrage if they took away the second-home allowance. What were people like him supposed to do, when they had constituencies miles away, in Dorset? If you pay peanuts you get monkeys, Rufus said.

Mrs. Armitage told her husband Larry every detail. How Stella had come rushing to the sacristy, her face ghostly white. Mary-Margaret's pink-sprigged knickers. She still could not work out what Mary-Margaret was doing. There was a chair toppled over by the altar, the altar cloth all twisted, a Tupperware bowl lying on the floor, a soapy sponge, a J-cloth. The oddest thing was the big smudge on the altar cloth, which looked like the print of a hand that had been dipped in paint. Or blood. There had been a quantity of blood seeping from Mary-Margaret's head but, as she had said reassuringly to Stella and Father Diamond, you would expect that; head wounds always bled a lot. How, though, had Mary-Margaret managed to get blood on the cloth as well? Had she staggered up after she had fallen and grabbed the cloth before crashing down again? If she had, there would surely be spots of blood all over the shop. Well, it was a mystery, but not an especially entertaining one; not one to mull over in her mind for long. Mrs. Armitage had fetched a fresh altar cloth from the sacristy and taken the stained one home to wash.

In the small brick presbytery behind the church, Father Diamond ate the supper his housekeeper had left for him—peppered mackerel and coleslaw. Tonight was a rare night, without parish commitments; he supposed he would go to bed early, make up for much-needed sleep. But once he was in bed, sleep mocked him, playing catch-me-if-you-can and slipping from his grasp just when he thought he'd caught it. He was constantly surprised by how alert the mind could stay when the body was expecting sleep. And the senses too; each magnifying the elements in its particular orbit. The wind, which in truth could not be much more than a breeze, became a gale, the sound of the traffic on Battersea Bridge a roar. The light from the streetlamp outside that edged his window blind was too bright for his eyes. In the morning, when his alarm clock woke him, his bed would be comfortable but now it felt as if the sheets were made of fiberglass and the pillow stuffed with stones. He tried every trick he knew to entrap sleep. Keeping one's eyes wide open in the dark was said to be infallible, but it never worked for him. Tensing every muscle in the body slowly, starting with the toes of the right foot and working upward to the face before relaxing all of them in one swift rush was another recommended fail-safe. But Father Diamond found it only made him conscious of his body. So he tossed and wriggled, and meanwhile his mind whirred on and on like a machine with a faulty off switch.

Thank the Lord for Mrs. Armitage, he thought. She was so reliable, turning up every Thursday morning with her mops and buckets, carting home stained albs and altar cloths, returning them the next week in piles as crisp and clean as newly fallen snow. And asking for nothing in return, except for conversation, which, it must be said, tended to be prolonged. But, even so, salt of the earth. Good of her to clean up all the mess in the Souls Chapel: what could that silly woman have been doing? If Mrs. Armitage was a right chatterbox, Stella Morrison was an icon of silence. The sunlight streaming down on her, and her arms full of flowers. Stella, he said out loud. He loved the sound of that word. Stella maris. Mater admirabilis, rosa mystica. Stella.

No one thought of telling Mary-Margaret's mother that her daughter was in hospital until Mary-Margaret herself came round to her full senses at about six o'clock that evening. Fidelma O'Reilly answered the telephone beside the armchair in which she had sat all day. She might as well stay there, she thought. It was too late to be facing all that kerfuffle on her own. Hauling herself out of the armchair, reaching her bedroom, sloughing off the outer layer of clothes. No, there was no point; she might as well stay where she was till morning. She had everything that she might need. A flask of tea, a packet of chocolate-covered digestive biscuits, her Winstons. She sat wedged in her chair and looked out of the window over the streets of Battersea to Wandsworth, where darkness had long fallen. Across the way a tower block, the twin of hers; columns and rows of rectangular windows, lit up like bisected screens. People going about their lives behind them. Fidelma leaned forward to unlatch her own window and push it open. It did not open very far. She knew why: imagine if all the people in all these blocks were able to throw their windows wide and stand upon their sills, rocking slowly back and forward on their heels while the London traffic crawled beneath them and beneath them too the wheeling gulls. No, she could see why the windows were designed to let in no more than an inch or two of outside air. But it was air enough. Up here on the nineteenth floor, with the window open, the wind blew in like a housebreaker, searching underneath the chairs to find what might be hidden there, lifting the curtains in case someone stood behind them. It rustled through the pages of the *Radio Times* as if it needed to read them in a hurry. Fidelma saluted the wind. At home it had been her daily companion, although there it was at the level of the ground. Brothers and sisters the winds must be, a whole gang of them, scouring the world for lost things, like the children of Lir. With the strong wingbeats of swans. When they fly overhead, the swans, no sound then but their wings. And that a sound so surprising in its loudness. Thunder almost. Swans and wind. The winds were the same winds all through time, all through the world. Born when the world was made, trapped by it like wild birds in bell glass, their wings forlornly beating, forced to roam around it until the end of time.

*

In St. Elizabeth's Hospital, Mary-Margaret lay in bed, with stitches in her scalp. Every hour, on the hour, a night nurse woke her. What month is this? she asked. Do you know your postcode? Who is the Prime Minister? Mary-Margaret had been extremely lucky, the nurses and the doctor said. She had cut her head, apparently, on the sharp edge of the tiled step leading to the altar, but it was a flesh wound merely, nothing graver; no fracture or serious damage. Mild concussion. She would be none the worse for it. Her wrist was broken, though, where she had fallen on it, and she was badly bruised. Best to stay there for a day or two, rest and recover, then she'd be as right as rain. Meanwhile Mary-Margaret was still a bit confused. What had happened just before her fall? She could not quite remember but images came back to her: a bleeding head, clear eyes looking into hers. She tried to tell the nurses who floated in and out of her dreams, but mostly they just hushed her: rest now, dear, they said. After all, this patient was concussed. Only one of them, Kiti Mendoza, stopped to listen. She had heard that this fat woman had been brought to hospital from a church. He opened his eyes, the woman was saying. He looked at me. His head was bleeding but it wasn't my fault. Really, it was not my fault.

Stella Morrison also lay in bed, listening to her husband breathe. His snuffling joined the other noises of the night; an open sash window rattling in the wind, a motorcycle in the distance, the sighing branches of the silver birch outside. Often sleepless, Stella was in the habit of wandering around the house at night, moving in the darkness through the empty rooms. It was a habit born in the days when her children were still small and she, a light sleeper like all mothers, would wake at the slightest sound. Then, she would have gone into their bedrooms to kneel beside them, to listen to the rhythm of their dreams. She would know if the dreams were calm or hectic by their bedclothes, tangled round them or composed. Felix in particular spent heated nights; his hair was often wet with sweat, and she'd stroke it off his forehead, breathing in the sweet small-boy scent of him, her sleeping child.

If the children had ever woken to find her there beside them, would they have felt she was intruding? She thought not: they would simply have accepted her presence in the night as they did during the day, unquestioned as the source of all they wanted, trivial or large. Besides, it is difficult to wake a sleeping child.

At that time she would have welcomed the quiet of the night. The voices of children had filled every minute of the day; there was never time to think her own thoughts or repair the raveled threads of life. After she had tucked the kicked-off duvets back and kissed her children lightly, she would often go from room to room, straightening rugs and cushions, putting toys away, making neat piles of the books and papers Rufus always scattered. That way she could greet the next day with lightness in her mind. Imposing order brought repose. She was familiar with the night sounds then; the creakings and the rus-tlings, the intermittent humming of the fridge, the sudden twang the piano sometimes made as if a ghost inside its case had plucked a string, occasionally a hunting owl. There would be all the same sounds now in the further reaches of the house but tonight she did not care to meet them. These unpeopled spaces, which usually seemed quite kindly, tonight threatened to unsettle; there was too much emptiness in them. For no clear reason she found herself thinking of the palaces of extinct kings. Fortresses on the crowns of hills, as large as towns, like labyrinths or termite mounds, the inner depths a honeycomb of rooms, jewel-embedded marble, windowless. Lost courtyards in which lonely women hid. Stella had got completely lost in the hill palace of Udaipur on her honeymoon with Rufus. One minute Rufus had been there, taking photographs and batting away the touting guides, the next minute he was not. She was in a narrow roofless space with doors at each corner opening onto spiral staircases, where the only light came filtered through fretworked pale stone. She chose the stairs she hoped would lead her in the same direction she and Rufus had been following; he must have gone on without her; she would find him at the top. But at the top there was only a narrower room lit by one dim bulb and she no longer knew whether to go left or right. She felt the panic of a lost child, of a dreamer in a hostile and strange city. This unimaginably complicated place was a maze, a prison; designed as such by one beleaguered ruler after another, each one insisting on his own accretions until there could be no one living who had kept count of all the rooms. It was all too easy to envisage being trapped in one and beating as ineffectually as a moth against the solid wood and brass inlay of its heavy door.

"The spider weaves the curtains in the palace of the Caesars; the owl calls the watches in the towers of Afrasiab," Stella said under her breath. The women of the emperors and the sultans: had they found consolation in the scarlet petals of the roses in their secret gardens, in the soft breath of a sleeping child?

Some nights, when she could not sleep, Stella got out of bed and crossed the landing to Barnaby's room, untenanted in term-time. It faced onto the street and there was a street-lamp right outside, beyond the railings, which turned mist into gold on autumn nights, made raindrops bright as fire-flies. Stella would lean her head against the glass, feeling its coldness, watching her breath cloud it, sensing the London smell of dust. If she closed her eyes and counted to ten before she opened them again, he would be standing on the pavement looking up, his collar turned against the damp, in a mandorla of light. Who he was she never knew, only that she needed him to be there.

The next day was a Friday. Fidelma O'Reilly was woken by the need to pee. She had been drifting in and out of dreams for what seemed like hours and in those dreams there had been toilets with locked doors, corridors that she was lost in, until finally she let go luxuriously of a great cascading stream. Fidelma's dreams often contained a bursting blad-der. Of late she had begun to fear that the release which was so carefree in her dreams might signify a real event; that there would come a morning when she would waken to a mattress stained and stinking, wet sheets already cool-ing as she slept.

But this morning she woke in her chair. It took her a bit of time to hoist herself out of it and stand up. Her legs were cramped and stiff. Hold on, my darling, she said aloud to herself. Get a good grip on yourself down there, my girl.

In the bathroom she pulled up her skirt and plopped down onto the specially adapted lavatory seat. Long ago she had dispensed with underwear; the elastic gouged red tracks on her skin and there was no call for that. When she had finished she shivered involuntarily and wondered, not for the first time, why that happened. Little girls shivered every time they went; she remembered that. It was a sort of pleasure, she supposed, that warm flow of liquid running from the secret places. One of the best, now she came to think of it: there was nothing like the relief of going when you really had to, like thirst it was; it's worth working up a real thirst just for the pleasure of its quenching. Sometimes she'd let her throat grow dry as the last scrapings of a scuttle before she drank cool water down.

A picture came to mind of a thirsting man, beads of sweat like teardrops, well-toasted from the sun. Lifting a tall glass full of Guinness to his mouth. You could see how cold the glass was from the frost upon it, you could see the way the young man's Adam's apple went a-bobbing up and down, the way a young fellow drains a pint without stopping for a breath, or so it seems. Had she once been acquainted with this young man, or was he off the telly?— these days she found it hard to know. There was a young man in an ad, but that was for Coke not Guinness, he was a builder or some such, a nice flat belly and the lasses crowding at an office window, craning for a look. Ah well.

Fidelma rinsed out a flannel in the washbasin and mopped at her face, her neck and armpits. Then she maneuvered herself into the kitchen. There was just enough space in it for her to stand between the counter and the cooker and, if she stepped to one side, she could open the fridge. What with Mary-Margaret not coming home last night, there might not be much in it. Mary-Margaret would have stopped off at the shops on her way back. But Fidelma had forgotten there was still most of a pork pie in there, some cooked potatoes, eggs and half a loaf. She put some lard into a pan and fried up the potatoes. When they were done, she pushed them to one side of the pan with a wooden spoon, added another lump of lard and fried two eggs as well. While they were doing, she spread margarine on a slice of bread.

That doctor of hers was forever going on about what Fidelma should be eating, or, more to the point, what she should not. Diet, diet, diet, she was sick of the stupid word. It was not by chance that if you took the *t* off it, you'd get its close relation. Anyway. Not even that interfering woman—and she was so scrawny that if she were a chicken she'd be fit for nothing but the stockpot—could complain about the meal Fidelma had made herself today. Meat, eggs and potatoes, that was all she'd ever eaten as a child, near enough, and then she was as slender as a reed, as the tall leaves of the yellow irises that grew in the boggy places, and had stayed so, until Mary-Margaret came along.

Fidelma took her plate of food back to her armchair, and ate it looking out of the window. It was late morning; children who went to school were long gone, and those of the parents who had work as well. There was not much happening below. If Mary-Margaret had been there, they would have watched the telly, but left to herself Fidelma could not be bothered to turn it on. She'd rather sit there with her food, savoring the salt taste of the pie jelly and then its rich fat melting on her tongue, thinking her own thoughts and minding her own business. Later she would brew some tea and have a cigarette but she'd wait a while for that; the waiting made the first drag so much better. The raisin scent of the fag unlit, that small white tube of promise and then the almost painful rush of it into the lungs; well, all in all, with a brew of tea, that would be just about enough.

As it was a Friday, Father Diamond spent most of the morning on the wards of St. Elizabeth's. As usual he collected his list of Roman Catholic patients from the cheerful lady in the Welfare Office and as usual she greeted him: how's tricks then, Rev? At the bottom of the list he was annoyed to notice Mary-Margaret O'Reilly but he'd have to look in on her, he knew he could hardly miss her out. He would leave her until last, after he had visited the seriously sick where they lay on the surgical wards.

Father Diamond had been an ordained priest for less than a year when his Superior added hospital chaplaincy to his list of duties. At first he had found it very hard. It was not the dying he minded, on the threshold of eternal life. No, for that he had had some training and besides it was precisely because he must learn to face the infinite that he had decided, after years of torment, to become a priest. To kneel beside the dying, to pray with them and at the end to bring them the precious consolation of the sacraments; well that was a blessing and a God-given privilege. But it was the naked way in which some of them were dying that upset him. The reek of advanced illness, all those tubes and pumps full of vile liquid, the yellow and the red, the mottled flesh, the ulcers, the indignity, the crusts of spittle, the toothlessness; all of this he found repellent. And he knew that he was wrong to do so. *Humani nil a me alienum puto* was the line that kept coming back to him but, as he often reflected ruefully, those self-righteous souls who cited it so glibly less often prefaced it with its true opening words: *Homo sum.*

Father Diamond knew that nothing human was foreign to God. The sores of lepers, the stumps of amputees—God saw them, loved them and would not hesitate to stroke them with His hands. When Lazarus stumbled out into the daylight from the darkness of his tomb, putrid and stinking to high heaven, having lain for four days dead, Jesus clasped him to His breast. (Who, though, would have peeled off his winding cloths, sticky with the liquefaction of the body in the heat of Bethany? Not Our Lord, thought Father Diamond. Martha, most probably. And then she would have laundered them for further use.) But it was all very well for God. And for those saints on earth who tended suppurating wounds and wiped the black froth from the mouths of the plague-ridden without flinching. Such mortals had the protection of their certain faith. Human though they were, they were also touched by the divine. For ordinary men and women it was natural to shrink away from the impure. Father Diamond had read his behavioral science and he knew that disgust was a primordial reflex; the species maximizing its own chances of survival by avoiding sources of infection and disease. *Homo sum,* and for that very reason I am nauseated by decaying flesh.

All Father Diamond could do was pray for strength. And so he did, until by now, eleven years after he had been appointed one of the several chaplains at St. Elizabeth's, he was much less squeamish. Even so, there were sights that still made him gag and served starkly to remind how far he was from sainthood.

Today Father Diamond visited a middle-aged man on the genitourinary ward, two ladies in gynae and a young man who had a tumor in his jaw. To remove it, the surgeons had also to remove some of his face and now there was a hole where bone had been before. He also went to see a man who had been dying for some time and had already received Extreme Unction. Father Diamond made the sign of the cross over him in blessing. Then he set off to find Mary-Margaret O'Reilly.

She was on a general ward, in the middle of a row of beds. Father Diamond was glad to see that she was sitting up and draped decently in a hospital-provided nightdress. How are you, dear? he asked.

Her face lit up. I'm doing well, Father, she said. I'm sorry for the trouble.

No trouble at all, he answered. The thing is that you're on the mend. Nothing broken, I trust?

My wrist, said Mary-Margaret. But only that. And a bit of bruising. But much worse things happen on a big ship, don't they?

They do indeed. You are very lucky. We should give thanks and praise to our good Lord.

I do and all, she said. And I say sorry to Him too, although it was not my fault. I promise I was gentle. I did not mean to hurt Him. It was not my fault.

What do you mean, Mary-Margaret? Father Diamond asked.

Well you know what I mean, she said. The wounds on His poor head. The blood. When He opened his eyes I could see how badly He was hurting and I'd have given anything to take away the pain.

There were no wounds, said Father Diamond gently. The blood was from *your* head. And from the look of things that's mending nicely. No need for vinegar and brown paper!

Mary-Margaret looked puzzled. She had no idea what he meant. Vinegar? She let it pass; Father Diamond was prone to saying strange things, she found. But now he must be made to see the truth. There was, she said. Blood. From the holes made by the thorns. It went all over my hands when I was anointing Him. With the olive cream.

My dear, said Father Diamond. You have had a big bump and a nasty shock into the bargain. Please don't worry any more. The cross is fine, nothing was broken. Mrs. Armitage will wash the altar cloth. Just you concentrate on getting better. We need you back on Thursday afternoons! Mrs. Armitage is made of sterling stuff but even she can't manage the cleaning by herself, we need both of our Stakhanovites!

More riddles, Mary-Margaret said to herself, and suddenly she felt too weary to explain. She'd show Father Diamond when she was back on her feet, she thought; it would be better if he saw it for himself. Meanwhile she accepted his blessing and the light touch of his hand on hers before he walked away.

❃

Kiti Mendoza, on the Friday evening shift, pulled up a chair beside the fat woman's bed and asked how she was doing. Well enough, the woman said, except her wrist was hurting. But you were fortunate, said Kiti, from what I heard. You could of broken your back. It must have been an angel stopped you fall. Oh no, said Mary-Margaret. I know it was Our Lord. He didn't manage quite to stop me falling altogether—it happened very quickly—but He caught me before I did myself any real harm. I could've died, you know, it was a long way down. What was you doing there? Kiti asked, and Mary-Margaret told her. The open eyes, the bleeding wounds, the certainty of love.

Early on Saturday morning, Stella and Rufus Morrison drove down from Battersea to their house in his constituency. Stella packed food for the weekend in a cool box; there would be no time for shopping. Rufus had his surgery to take, meetings with his agent, with the Master of the local hunt who was campaigning for the repeal of unpopular legislation, and with the chairman of the parish council; there was also a fund-raising dinner to attend that night. Some kind of competition—she had forgotten what—to adjudicate on Sunday morning, and then they would have to drive back to London so that the whole week's round could begin again—Shadow Cabinet meetings, off-the-record briefings, debates and argument, Select Committees, jostlings for airtime—Rufus's round, all underpinned by Stella.

There was one small break in Saturday's program that Stella was anticipating with the pleasure she had known when she first met Rufus. He had been married to someone else then, his secret hours with Stella stolen out of a shared and busy life. They used to meet in the back room of a pub in Dean Street, and Stella remembered the ardor she felt as she hurried toward it, the ecstasy of being sure that in a moment she would be with the man who filled her waking thoughts and her better dreams. That ecstasy must have been visible in some way, she later thought; strangers stopped what they were doing and turned to look at her rushing past them on Shaftesbury Avenue; men, with hungry eyes.

So many years ago, and now Stella was longing for a meeting not with a lover but with her youngest child. It would be too brief—these meetings always were—and she'd pay for it with an hour of cold on a soggy sports pitch, but he'd be there, his aliform shoulder blades, his muddy knees, the ravishment of his smile. How was it possible, she thought, to miss anyone as painfully as she missed him? Even in the most fervid time of her affair with Rufus, when every parting felt as if a layer were being cruelly torn from her vulnerable heart, she had known that she could bear the hours that followed. But this? This was sorrow of a different kind. A dull but unremitting throb that was the pulse of every day in term time.

Rufus drove. He always drove, except after dinner parties. He did not want to talk; he was listening to a disc his secretary had recorded of an important speech made at the Confederation of British Industries. Stella contemplated his hands, resting on the steering wheel; long fingers with protuberant knucklebones, a feathering of light brown hair over the outer metacarpals. An edge of tattered check cuff showing beneath his navy sweater; his tweed jacket on the backseat; a weekend shirt, working weekend clothes. Hands were so strangely intimate, she thought, and yet they were the one part of the human body that was always on display. Even where women have their faces covered, they are allowed to bare their hands. Hands that have known the inner places of the body; their own, their children's and their lovers'. She had looked at the hands of men holding knives and forks at a dinner table—fat hands and slim ones, stubby-fingered, hairy—and envisaged their profound acquaintance with the bodies of their wives, who sat a conventional distance away round the same table. Rufus's hand recognized the contours of her breasts so easily, he'd probably ceased to register them as things apart. Stella's body had become his property through the rights of ownership accumulated over years of marriage.

The M3, the A303, past Andover, through Sherborne. A route so tediously familiar she barely noticed the landmarks. But she did notice the changes every week in the hedgerows and the waysides, those reminders of the fields and hills that had been there before the roads tore strips from them and left their green flanks scarred. That Saturday morning, in late March, winter skeletons were beginning to be touched by green, pale sunlight flickered throughout translucent leaves. Wild cherry flowering everywhere, cherry like drifting snow. On the blackthorn, tender and beautiful white blossom, as delicate as a bride's veil, and as hopeful. The bravery of these ancient trees, opening the paths to new sap every year, putting forth their youthful flowers. The white flowers of the thorn. The green of infant leaves so tentative they looked like mist on the bare branches, not solid form.

Saturday was Kiti's day off. She slept late, then called her friend Melinda. She mentioned the woman on the ward who believed she had reopened Our Lord's wounds. Kiti knew the church she had been talking about, on the corner of Riverside Crescent. Melinda said that was a little bit interesting; they should go and take a look. What else was there to do on a rainy Saturday in London, when you were trying to save money? Both girls were very homesick.

The Sacred Heart was open, as it was every day from eight till six. It was a point of pride and of principle to Father Diamond and his Superior, Father O'Connor, to allow unfettered access to the church. You could never tell when a soul in need might seek the presence of the Blessed Sacrament, Father O'Connor always said, even though it meant the devil to pay in insurance premiums. True, there were more often homeless people escaping from the rain in there than bona fide prayers, but they too were souls in need, of course, and who knows if they might find the Lord even though they were only seeking shelter?

There was no one in the church that Saturday afternoon. Kiti and Melinda crossed themselves with Holy Water from the stoup, genuflected and set off to find the cross that the fat woman had talked about. There were all the old familiar figures in the church: St. Joseph in his brown cloak, the Virgin in her blue dress, Jesus with his heart exposed. The cross hanging from the ceiling in front of the altar had no body on it, so clearly it was not the one they wanted. Eventually they located it in one of the two side chapels. A crucifix nailed to the wall above a narrow altar; Jesus in colored plaster.

With no natural light, the little chapel was very dim. Kiti and Melinda felt around for a light switch but they couldn't find one. Melinda suggested taking one of the candles from the wooden tray in front of the statue of Our Lady; Kiti put a 5p coin in the collection tin. A box of matches had been thoughtfully provided. Kiti struck one and held it to the candlewick while Melinda screened the new flame with her hand. Melinda carried the candle to the chapel and raised it to the crucifix. It flickered in the darkness, throwing the shadows of the two girls across the wall. They could just make out the silver reliquaries behind locked bars in niches in the wall, a painting to one side of a figure they could not identify. The pink legs and feet of God. But there was no blood. Kiti and Melinda were disappointed. Although what more could one expect from a silly Englishwoman who had given herself a big blow on the head? Then Kiti screamed. And Melinda too. Oh God, they screamed together. Did you see that? It was far too frightening. Melinda dropped the candle and they both fled from the church.

Felix Morrison spotted his mother hurrying across the pitch and felt a small constriction in his heart. She was late and the under-elevens were already being thrashed, as usual, having missed their first conversion and a penalty kick. But that wouldn't worry his mother, she never seemed to mind whether the team won or lost. In fact, she never even seemed to know which side was winning or losing until the match ended and the victors cheered. Felix had tried to explain the rules to her a hundred times but she still got them muddled up. The important thing is that you enjoy yourself and do your best, she had told him once, and he had not wanted to upset her with the truth, which was that winning really mattered. In the harsh world of his boarding school no amount of motherly solace could save a boy from being a loser.

In keeping with custom, Felix only nodded curtly to his mother when she reached the touchline, and ran past her after a disappearing ball. She gave him a little wave. That she was there, though, that she'd made it when he hadn't been sure she'd be able to, gave Felix a rush of strength, as if the sluggish blood in his veins had all of a sudden been displaced by something warmer and more pure. Ichor, he said to himself under his breath. The clear fluid that flowed in the veins of gods. The horrible hard ball was now cannoning toward him and could not be evaded unless Felix were to turn tail and head in the opposite direction. With the strength of heroes flooding through him, Felix lunged for it, grabbed it and ran for the tryline.

Stella kept her eyes trained on her child as he was tackled, stopped breathing as he disappeared beneath the ruck, breathed again when he emerged, without the ball but with his nose unbloodied. This barbarous pursuit, she thought, why do we do such terrible things to our sons? Rufus had been a rugger Blue at Oxford.

Some of the under-elevens, who could, apparently, be almost twelve, were nearly as tall as men and growing bulky.

Felix was by far the smallest of the team, a child so thin you might think you saw the gleam of bone through his white skin. A child made of lines and angles, the nape of his neck heartbreaking, his new front teeth like trespassers in his mouth. When the game was over he ran across to Stella. She looked beautiful, he noted, as she always did, much nicer-looking than the other mothers. She knew not to kiss him. Match tea, he said, I'm sorry, Mum. We have to have it with the visiting team. That's fine, she said. I hope it's good. You must be starving after all that brilliant playing.

I am, said Felix. It's a bit less than two weeks, I think, to the end of term?

That's right. About ten days, she said. I'll see you then. He nodded quickly and turned back to his team, now streaming off toward the changing rooms. She watched him go, yearning after him, the mud-stained hollows behind his fragile knees.

Father Diamond, readying the church for Saturday's vigil mass, saw the candle lying on the floor outside the Chapel of the Holy Souls. People can be so careless, he said to himself. The candle was no longer burning but it had evidently been lit; it could have caused a fire. He picked it up and stuck it in the stand.

There were eleven worshipers that evening, not bad for a Saturday in London, and Seamus was there to serve. Afterward, Father Diamond asked him to help with the Lenten veils. They were difficult to manage on one's own. Seamus, who also served on weekdays, was too shaky to be really helpful, but it was good to have an extra pair of hands.

Together the two men fetched the stepladder from the garage behind the house. Father Diamond had already taken the shrouds out of the cardboard boxes in which they were stored for the rest of the year and had heaped them in the sacristy. Heavy, thick material, a little faded at the folds, a little dusty; redolent of charity shops with their scent of mildew.

He and Seamus worked systematically, carrying the ladder between them. Our Lady and St. Joseph; the Sacred Heart, which was a statue Father Diamond disliked intensely but dared not upset his congregation by discarding; the crucifix in the Holy Souls. The cross that hung from the ceiling above the sanctuary was always the hardest to cover; too high for Father Diamond to reach with ease, and the material would keep slipping off. Eventually he managed to secure it with safety pins.

It was dark now, and the violet coverings made it seem darker still. Always such a bleak time for Father Diamond, the flowers gone, the statues shrouded like corpses in their cerements, like possessions under dust sheets in an abandoned house. His foot was on the top rung of depression; if he did not hold on fast he would slip down so far it would take enormous strength to clamber up. He was not sure that he could find the strength again. Before him stretched the final weeks of Lent: Palm Sunday, Maundy Thursday, the terror of Good Friday, agony and passion, tallow candles and the altar bare.

I don't know what I'd do without you, Seamus, he said truthfully. How about a drink, or are you rushing off this evening? Seamus made the sideways movement of his head that expressed regret more courteously than a straight refusal. Thanks a million, Father, but there's things I should be doing. Fine, said Father Diamond, bless you.

Stella did not stay for tea with the other parents after Felix's match but sped off to get herself ready for the evening. It was desolating to drive away from the school and out through its iron gates, leaving her child behind. Stella had heard other women tell of times when they had forgotten their children in playgrounds and shopping centers; there had been a family recently in the news who were halfway across the Atlantic on a plane before they realized their four-year-old was missing. Stella had laughed in the approved manner at these comic instances of the softening effect of motherhood on the brain but was privately appalled. When her children were small she had felt as if the cords that once connected them to her were still in place; she was as aware of them as her own heartbeat, her own breath.

Barnaby and Camilla had made their own graceful adjustments to the umbilical ties; stretching them to encompass nights away at first, and later weeks, then holidays with friends, and finally the long intervals of their gap years and university. Camilla at that very moment was in the north of Thailand, near the Burmese border, teaching English to the children of Karen refugees. Barney had spent a year traveling in South America and was now at Cambridge. It had been agony, of course, to let them go. When she waved Barney good-bye at Heathrow Airport, she had felt terribly afraid that it would be forever. At the back of her wardrobe was Camilla's nightdress, discarded on her bed when she went to Thailand. A faded gray thing, an old favorite, it had reached Camilla's ankles when it was new and now it skimmed her thighs. Like a frugal addict, Stella allowed herself to bury her face in it, to breathe in its scent, only at the times when she most acutely missed her daughter. As the months went by, the scent was getting fainter. Stella worried a little, and knew she was quite mad for doing so, about its laundering. To wash it before Camilla came home safely would be to court disaster. But if she waited, Camilla would know, and think her mother sentimental.

Rufus was at the front door of the house when she got there, leaning against the jamb, listening to an elderly man in tweed whom Stella did not recognize. You know my wife, of course? said Rufus, and the man said that he did. Won't you come in for a cup of tea? Stella asked him, and then caught Rufus's warning look. Luckily the visitor said he must get home, he still had to wash the dogs.

Thank God for that, Rufus said, when the man had finally taken his leave. He's got to be the biggest bore in Christendom. What were you doing, asking him in for tea? Anyway, I still have calls to make—what time are we on parade?

Seven for 7:30, Stella said, wondering if there was enough time for her to prune the ceanothus that grew along one wall of the garden. Toward the end of spring its fallen flowers would drift like flakes of dark blue paint, of lapis lazuli, across the paving stones. If she were not there at the right time, Stella would miss them—their intense blue against the gray stone, the white clouds of bridal wreath still flowering about them. Too often she missed the ephemeral events of this garden which she saw only at weekends, and felt that she neglected. There was a climbing rose for instance, so briefly in bloom that it was like Bishop Berkeley's tree: if it flowered unseen, could it be said to flower at all?

This was the house that Rufus had bought when he knew he had been selected to stand for the safe seat of Central Dorset. Nothing ostentatious, he had stipulated beforehand. Something comfortable, in a village, something that would put him at the heart of the community.

And so this rather beautiful old house with its walled garden and a mulberry tree. A passage led straight from the front door to the back; when both doors were open on a bright day it became a corridor of light. The roof beams were hundreds of years old. In one room, now converted to a kitchen, were the remains of an ancient anvil; when Rufus bought it the house was called Ye Olde Forge. He had officially renamed it 32 Middle Street, but the children still called it the Forgery. Their possession of it was a little fraudulent, Stella sometimes felt. For the generations who had lived there it had represented permanence, a place of work, a settled place in life. The house next door had been a bakery, the one beyond, built a little later, was still called the Old Bank. Now there was nowhere in the village where a person could earn a living except as a cleaner or an odd-job man. Or, of course, as an MP. Rufus's office was in the house; during surgery hours on Saturdays his constituents straggled up the path with their anxieties and complaints, their health and housing problems. Or simply because they needed proof that he was there in person. Rufus was good at what he did.

Darkness was falling too fast to allow for any pruning, Stella realized. Tomorrow the clocks would go forward and there would be a precious extra hour of light that evening, the start of a gentle progress toward nights when it would not be necessary to draw the curtains and light the lamps against the dark. Today, though, Stella could still feel the touch of winter in the damp stone walls and in the silence of the birds that were also waiting for renewed light, and the morning.

An unsettling aspect of life in this old house was that there was seldom anything in it for Stella to do, except the gardening. That, she had chosen—it was not a difficult garden to look after, being small and stone-flagged and containing nothing delicate or rare. But Linda from the other end of the village came in twice a week to keep things clean, and any other routine jobs were dealt with by Rufus's constituency secretary, who summoned plumbers and electricians as required, and sent their bills on to the House of Commons. Stella had never even needed to change a lightbulb. It was, she thought, like living in the sort of hotel whose barely visible management pretended it was an ordinary home.

Now she wandered through the sitting room and the kitchen, wanting something, but not knowing what that was. She picked up the book that she had been reading— Elizabeth Taylor's first novel—and put it down again. She wondered about telephoning a friend. By then it was after six; she could legitimately suppose that it was time to change for dinner.

Almost all of Stella knew exactly what that evening had in store. But a fraction of her could still feel faintly hopeful.

Interesting people turned up in the least likely of places, even at a dinner in a nearby country house held in support of an appeal to raise money for the local staghounds. She and Rufus had to be there; he was a great friend of the host's and, besides, he was in favor of the Countryside Alliance.

Dressing for the evening has a ritual quality about it, Stella thought. As for a priestess in an Attic temple preparing for sacrifice, there were ceremonial adornments to put on in a special order. She looked at herself carefully in the bathroom mirror. Brushing shadow onto her eyelids, underlining them with charcoal gray, she saw a face that did not entirely fit her own. Something had been lost behind those dark-fringed eyes but she did not know what it was.

That night, a little later, Mary-Margaret O'Reilly accepted a cup of tea from a ward assistant and stretched out luxuriously in her bed. Beneath her the white cotton sheet slithered against the plastic-covered mattress. She had seen the doctor, who had said she could go home. Her head was mending well and the nurse at her local GP practice could take her stitches out next week. Her wrist needed only to be kept strapped up. The doctor had sounded jolly and encouraging, sure that he was the bringer of good news. Mary-Margaret had not the heart to tell him she'd much rather stay where she was for the next week or so. She liked the companionship of the mixed ward, the old fella who always stopped at the foot of her bed to pass the time of day on his way to and from the toilets; Myrna, who knew the secrets

of so many celebrated hearts—film stars and football play-
ers' wives and that girl who was on *Big Brother*—and had,
in addition, the blessing of a great many cheerful grandchildren who brightened up the place no end. She liked the
high and narrow bed and its white-painted bars. She liked
being given a jug of water with a special lid. It was a very
pleasant change to have her meals served to her, food that
she had neither had to buy nor to cook. She liked the gravy,
thick and shiny as melted caramel, the pats of butter like
little bars of treasure in their wrappings of gold. No, she
was not yet ready to give these comforts up. Of course she
burned to be with Him again. But at the same time she felt
a curious need to let more time elapse. When Sister came
round in the morning, Mary-Margaret decided, she would
tell her how badly her head pained her and how she really
should be left to rest.

In another narrow bed, this one the bottom half of a bunk,
Felix Morrison was thinking about British Summer Time.
Spring forward, fall back. In the middle of the night he
would lose a whole hour of his life, but that didn't really
add up to much, if you did the maths. How many hours
had he lived already? Twenty-four times three hundred
and sixty-five times ten, and seven months—well, he
could do that in his head; just about, it came to ninety-
two thousand, six hundred, and forty, or something, but
then there were uneven months and leap years, how many
of those had there been in his lifetime? Years divisible by
four: 2000, 2004, 2008—add twenty-four times these.
Hold on, of course, you'd get the lost hours back when the

clocks changed again in winter. So maybe it was a pointless calculation after all. But it helped to pass the miserable hours of darkness and enforced confinement, when Felix so often lay awake while above and all around him other schoolboys slept. It was better to do sums than to remember the missed pass that afternoon and his captain's scorn at tea, or to count the minutes until the end of term, and home.

Father Diamond adjusted his watch first and then the clock on the mantelpiece in time to the chimes of the ten o'clock news. It was irritating that, although these two would now both be in time for this one moment, all the other clocks that had to be adjusted—the central heating, the radio alarm beside his bed, in the sacristy and in the church itself—would perforce be inaccurate, if only by a second or so. He watched the news. Swine flu, the recession, two more British soldiers killed in Afghanistan. "O the mind, mind has mountains," he quoted to himself. "Cliffs of fall." When the news was finished, he took his coffee cup into the kitchen and washed it. His house backed onto a high wall and beyond it was the river. It was quiet there at night.

Stella envisaged the darkness of the river and for a moment closed her eyes. All around her there was noise. Cutlery and glasses, shouted conversations and guffaws. The man on her left had turned to her during the main course with ill-disguised reluctance; she recognized his struggle to find something he could talk to her about. His kind was bored by women. I was at school with your husband, he said. But in a different house, of course, and possibly a year or two above. In the bad old days, Stella said brightly. Rufus says it is much better now. Since they stopped the canings.

Bloody stupid of them, if you ask me. Did us a world of good. That's the trouble now; no discipline. Lot of whingers and too many bleeding hearts. A good thrashing's part of growing up.

But surely you can't approve of children hitting other children? That's what happened, wasn't it? The prefects were allowed to do the canings—

What d'you mean, children? We weren't children, we were men. And a sight more decent than what passes for men in some quarters nowadays. Bring it all back, I say.

The street sounds of a Saturday night rose up toward Fidelma where she sat by her open window; muffled, because they were so far below; voices, motorbikes and music, the pulsing beat of rhythmic bass notes like a heart's thud heard within the womb. Drumbeats. Tribal drums, like jungle messages or the lambegs—was that the word?—those fellows that played them, with their bowler hats and gray-potato faces. It was queer, now that she thought about it, those stiff figures and their iron laws—Ulster Says No Surrender; Beware the Antichrist—and yet the same God-fearing fingers on the wild drumsticks, thudding out those urgent calls. Thump, thump, thump, they must be echoes, surely, of the pulse of heartbeats in the rhymes of love. Thump, thump, thump, and the bedsprings creaking, hush now or you'll wake the young ones up. But those men in their black hats, like versions of the wee fellows on the sacks of Homepride flour, those men and their marching, ah well, their thoughts were very far from love.

Fidelma ate the Fray Bentos steak pie that had been in the kitchen cupboard, and some beans. There was nothing much to drink but Bushmills. Stocks were getting low, but no doubt Mary-Margaret would be back before much longer. Fidelma supposed she would be glad to see her daughter. She was weary of sitting here in her own smells. The bass beats thudded out and she sat and heard them; she thought they echoed her own heart.

Stella and Rufus, coming home on Sunday evening, wondered what the crowd was doing, milling round the church at the end of the crescent. Must have been a wedding, Rufus said. Unlikely on a Sunday, Stella thought, but did not contradict him, her mind only on whether there would be an e-mail waiting from Camilla.

Father Diamond had also been surprised, much earlier in the day. Later he was cross. With Father O'Connor away, it was his duty to say both the Sunday masses. He had gone into the church via the sacristy, through the side door, at the end of the path which connected it to his house. He had not seen the knot of people gathered at the front.

So early in the morning it was dark. For a few moments Father Diamond stood stock-still in the darkness, encircled by the shrouded statues, breathing in grave scents of damp and stone and dust. A silent place, empty but for God. Then he switched on all the lights. Moving down the nave, straightening a pew that had been knocked out of alignment, he checked that all was as it should be before he, by sacramental grace, made God incarnate in that earthly space.

Father Diamond's early Sunday morning server, Major Wetherby, was late. The priest had to make the preparations by himself. In the sacristy he filled a cruet with wine and water and a ciborium with bread. He laid out his own vestments—alb, cincture, stole and chasuble—in the somber color of Lent. The linen was kept in the shallow drawers of an old oak press; he took what he needed from them—altar cloth and frontal, purifiers, another starched white cloth for the credence table. He readied a chalice. Then he went back into the church. He put the offerings in their place, and a missal on the credence table. There was a second table to the right for the bell and the vessel of water. The white cloths unfolded in his hands like a fall of sudden snow. Lastly he lit the candles on the altar.

It was 7:45. There was still no sign of Major Wetherby so Father Diamond took the great iron key from its hook beside the main door and opened the door himself. Before he had pushed it fully open, a throng of people jostled past him, shouldering him aside. Usually there were no more than a handful of worshipers at the early mass on Sunday; he had never seen a queue before. Looking at these people he saw that they were mainly women, mainly young, and also, possibly, foreign. Had he overlooked an important commemoration or a beloved patron saint's feast day? He couldn't think of one. He said good morning and went back to the sacristy.

Even now, after so many years, the final minutes before the start of every mass were touched by fear. Father Diamond knew the fear of a diver on the edge of a springboard, of a dancer in the wings waiting for his call. Each time, every single day, as he watched the minute hand, he would be gripped by dread: would he be able to walk through the sacristy door into the sanctuary; could he be confident of grace? It could be lonely, at the altar.

He vested, saying silent prayers. Lord, gird me about with the cincture of purity and extinguish my fleshly desires that the virtue of continence and chastity may abide within me. The chasuble was heavy on his shoulders. Stiff purple silk. 7:56. Major Wetherby came in through the side door, puffing. In the nick, he said. Top of the morning, Father. He put on his cassock and surplice hastily. Then both he and Father Diamond bowed their heads to the image of the Sacred Heart before Major Wetherby opened the door on the dot of 8:00 and clanged the bell. He led the way and Father Diamond followed, bearing the chalice covered with a purifier, a pall, a purple veil and a corporal folded in a matching burse.

Father Diamond kept his head bent over the precious chalice and his eyes lowered until he reached his place behind the altar. Then he looked up, anticipating the joyful sight of a sizable congregation, a change from the familiar few faces he was used to seeing. They were there, in their accustomed pews. But the others, the visitors, were not in the pews at all but, from the sound of it, gathered in the Chapel of the Holy Souls. Father Diamond waited for a minute to give them time to settle down. Perhaps they had not heard the bell. He cleared his throat. There was scant response. Two or three did detach themselves from the rest and slid into a pew. The others stayed where they were, mostly hidden from him. He got on with saying mass.

In the course of it he became irritably aware that the visitors were not only staying segregated in the chapel but also making quite a lot of noise. A prayerful noise certainly, some sort of litany perhaps, but other noises too: furniture scraping on the tiled floor, a great deal of excited chatter, the ring tones of mobile phones. More people kept arriving. Just before he began to say the Eucharistic Prayer he saw Miss Daly, a regular, bustle from her seat into the chapel. Voices were raised. Miss Daly returned to her pew, looking flustered and indignant. Father Diamond plowed on. He had no choice. It was a relief to see that a lot of the visitors did come up for Holy Communion. Some of them had covered their heads with lace.

When the mass was ended, Father Diamond followed Major Wetherby into the sacristy and started to disrobe. What the devil was all that about? Major Wetherby was asking, when there was a sharp knock at the door and Miss Daly came bristling in. Do come out at once and put a stop to all this nonsense, she demanded. Those stupid women are paying no heed to me at all. Father Diamond, struggling out of his alb, heard the note of outrage in her voice. He handed the garment to the major and followed Miss Daly to the chapel. There he found several women lying prostrate on the floor, others kneeling, and at least one apparently in tears. The altar was in disarray and the Lenten veil had been pulled off the crucifix. Every candle on the pricket stand was lit. O most holy blood of Jesus, a voice was chanting, over and over again. What is all this? Father Diamond asked. Who took off the veil? A woman detached herself from the group. You are blessed, she said. This place is going to be well famous.

Mary-Margaret, on Sunday morning, looked regretfully at the breakfast she would not allow herself to eat. Scrambled egg and button mushrooms. Triangles of toast. An hour ago she had tried to whiten her complexion with a little Ajax from a tin she had found on a windowsill in the bathroom but the grains were too coarse to stick. If anything, they made her redder. When an assistant came to take away her uneaten food, Mary-Margaret would not let her. It was important for the nurse in charge to see she could not take a bite.

But Sister, when she came, was angry with the assistant and not at all sympathetic to her patient. She looked at Mary-Margaret's wrist, listened to her account of the terrible pains that pierced her head, dispensed two acetaminophen and told her to get dressed. You're absolutely fine, dear, she said firmly. Take two acetaminophen, at no more than four-hourly intervals, if you need them, but do not exceed eight tablets a day. See your GP if you experience further problems. Don't forget to get those stitches taken out.

Mary-Margaret, forlorn, put on her pullover and her denim skirt. It was only then she noticed the bloodstains on the skirt. It looked bad, she knew, as if she'd had a shameful accident, but she had nothing else to wear. She could hardly make her way back home in a hospital nightie. It was lucky the ambulance men had had the wit to keep her united with her shopping bag and fleece. She got dressed slowly. Her wrist hurt and she couldn't do up her bra single-handed. Life wasn't fair, she thought.

It was still early and she had to wait a long time for a bus. While she waited, she tried to bring to mind what food there had been at home when she left on Thursday. She wondered what her mother had done about her meals. Now she wished she had eaten up that breakfast— she was feeling wobbly and, besides, her ploy had made no difference.

There was no direct bus route between her home and St. Elizabeth's. As Mary-Margaret would have to change buses in any case, she thought she might as well go via the Co-op. In the well-lit and warm shop she began to feel more cheerful. There were Cadbury's chocolate fingers on special offer, buy one, get one free. Thinking back to her uneaten breakfast she put eggs into her basket, a tin of mushrooms, a loaf and a packet of ham. A pint of milk to be on the safe side. A jar of sandwich spread. That would do for now, she felt. It was as much as she could carry. She could always go out again later, and get something else for tea.

The second bus came quickly. For such small mercies let us give thanks. But for some reason she could not quite identify, Mary-Margaret was in no hurry to get home. She could scarcely remember when she had last spent a night away from her mother. Her final summer at school, perhaps, when the nuns had arranged a trip to Normandy, to venerate the bones of St. Thérèse? Nearly all the fifth form went—they had stayed in the order's sister house. Oh, that had been a happy time. She remembered the journey there by train and ferry. The sea spray flying up toward her at the railing, the cold salt taste of it in her mouth. The feel of it came back to her now, and she wanted even less to shut herself up in the stinky, creaky lift of her tower block. Fidelma's great unmoving bulk spread like a black stain on her vision.

She decided instead to get a cup of tea from the takeout at the bottom of the block and drink it on the bench beside the children's play area. At that time on a Sunday morning, the area might well have children in it, rather than youths with drugs and dogs. There was even a glimmer of sunshine. After that, she'd see about dropping in on Him. Excitement fluttered through her at the thought.

She bought the tea with difficulty, it being hard to manage with her shopping on one arm. She had had to put everything down to rummage for her purse, and its clasp had proved well-nigh impossible. It does make you feel for the properly disabled, she observed to the man behind the counter, but he didn't seem to understand her, and only waited patiently while she fumbled for the coins. She would have liked him to inquire about her wrist and head.

In the broken-down play area there were children clambering on the roundabout and the swings. Mary-Margaret knew most of them. Among them were some of the many children of Mrs. Abdi, who lived on the same floor as the O'Reillys. So many, it was a struggle to tell them apart, but Mary-Margaret had made the effort. This morning she saw Hodan, Faduma, Sagal, Samatar, Bahdoon, and her favorite, the small one, Shamso, of the tight black curls. He was so sweet, that Shamso, with his great big eyes and his round cheeks, just like a gorgeous, cuddly doll. Today he was dressed in an odd array of hand-me-downs—jogging bottoms that were too big for him, a dirty T-shirt, and on top of that what looked like a ballerina costume. Pink nylon and pink netting, the shoestring straps slipping off his shoulders. Mary-Margaret took one of the packets of chocolate fingers from her bag. Shamso, she called, waving the packet at him. They all came, of course, and clustered round her but Shamso clambered up onto the bench beside her and snuggled against her side. She could feel his elbow, his little, pointy chin. Chocolate from his fingers added to the stains already on her skirt. But it didn't matter. It would all come out in the wash. Mary-Margaret put her good arm round him, drank her sweet, strong tea, shared her biscuit breakfast with the Abdis and raised her face to the pale sun that shone a tentative path between the tower blocks.

Mrs. Armitage and her husband arrived in good time for the solemn mass, the second mass of Sunday. They found the church door locked and a restive group of people gathered outside. They were perplexed. Maybe Father D has been called out to a deathbed, Mrs. Armitage speculated. It can't be easy for him on a Sunday, what with Father O'Connor away. Two masses, and that's not counting Saturday's, but still, it's not like him to shut the church. Especially not during Lent. Perhaps he's ill, her husband said. Oh no, said Mrs. Armitage. Not if I know him. He'd have to be on his own deathbed before he'd think of doing that. They eyed the waiting people curiously. They seemed a bit agitated. Girls on some sort of sightseeing thing, Mrs. Armitage told Larry. You know, one of those tours with all the stops prearranged. That must be why they're taking pictures. Although we're not usually on the tourist map. Their tour guide must've got it wrong, said Larry. Battersea and Westminster, well, they are both by the river. Maybe they sound the same in Japanese. Honestly, Larry! Mrs. Armitage clicked her tongue against her teeth.

Members of the regular congregation started to arrive. As they did, each one tried the door and looked surprised. Has he forgotten that the clocks changed? several asked. Mrs. Armitage began to fret that there would not be enough time to get out the hymnbooks. She caught sight of Mary-Margaret walking slowly up the road. Save us, she said to Larry, and at once regretted her lapse of charity. Poor Mary-Margaret. She meant no harm.

At five to eleven the door opened slightly and Father Diamond peered out. The tourists rushed toward him. Father Diamond barred their way with his arm. Visitors who genuinely wish to attend mass are most welcome, he said, with dignity. But this is a place of worship. Cameras and mobile phones are not allowed. The people at the front repeated his words to the others further back and there was an outburst of excited chatter. Okay, okay, a woman said. No problem.

Father Diamond opened the door wide and stepped back. As the visitors streamed past him, he was clearly looking for someone he recognized. Mrs. Armitage, he said gratefully, when he found her. On hymnbook and welcoming duty as usual? That's good. We seem to have a little problem in the second chapel so I have roped it off. I'd be awfully grateful if you and Larry could make sure no one tries to move the ropes. What's up then, Father? Larry asked, but Father Diamond pointed to his watch and hurried off.

Mr. and Mrs. Armitage observed that while a few of the visitors wandered around as if they were not sure what they were looking for and a few took places in the pews, most made straight for the Chapel of the Holy Souls. Father Diamond had lined up a row of chairs across the entrance, linking them together with string. Not an especially effective barricade, Mrs. Armitage said to herself. She busied herself with getting the hymnbooks off their shelf and into piles; it was annoying that all these new people had come in at once and hadn't stopped as regulars did to collect their books and service sheets. But at least, she noted approvingly, someone, probably Father D, had put the offerings and the collection plates on the right spot. Then she noticed that the woman who had spoken up on behalf of the group, and was a good bit older than the rest, was shunting the line of roped-up chairs aside to clear the chapel entrance. Larry! ordered Mrs. Armitage. He followed her pointing finger and turned back to her, looking a little helpless. But then, bravely, he marched off to the chapel and shunted the chairs back. The woman said something to him. Mrs. Armitage kept her eye on him approvingly as he answered, making gestures that clearly indicated where she and her friends were supposed to be if they wanted to hear mass. Taking his guard duty seriously, he sat squarely in the middle of the row of chairs. He was not an intimidating man, being small and narrow-chested. Mrs. Armitage decided that when the mass was under way, she had better station herself there too. First she must give out the hymnbooks.

Mary-Margaret shambled in, carrying a shopping bag. You're up and about, Mrs. Armitage greeted her. That's good. It was a very nasty cut you gave yourself, on your poor head. Mary-Margaret nodded. And I broke my wrist, she said. She wandered off, up the nave toward the front. Mrs. Armitage noted the stains all down her skirt. Par for the course, she thought.

The bell clanged, the organist struck an opening chord, Father Diamond came out, preceded by two boys with candles. The congregation rose. "Lord Jesus, think on me," they sang creakily. "And purge away my sin." Everyone seemed settled enough, thought Mrs. Armitage. Even the visitors. She allowed herself to relax into the well-known words and rhythms. Let us call to mind our sins, Father Diamond was saying. All her life Mrs. Armitage had been hearing words like these and responding to them with phrases so familiar she need give them no thought. I confess, she now said comfortably. These rituals fitted her as snugly as her wedding ring, as the navy blue cardigans that were her daily wear. The bells, the murmured prayers, the fragrant clouds of incense were the sounds and smells of home. Father Diamond announced the reading from the holy Gospel. Glory to you, Lord, answered Mrs. Armitage, making the sign of the cross with her right thumb on her forehead, lips and breast. "Jesus wept," read Father Diamond. "Still sighing, he reached the tomb: it was a cave with a stone to close the opening. Jesus said: Take this stone away. Martha said to him, Lord, by now he will smell. This is the fourth day.

Jesus replied, Have I not told you that if you believe me you will see the glory of God?"

You will see the glory of God, Mary-Margaret repeated under her breath, and her eyes burned with tears. But surely Martha was right, Mrs. Armitage thought, as she had often thought before. He would have stunk to high heaven, that brother of hers. She pictured Lazarus, staggering from the cave, his hands and feet bound with bands of stuff and a cloth round his face. The hot sun beating fiercely on the awestruck crowd.

Normally, when mass ended, it was Larry's task to gather up the hymnbooks and service sheets and to make things tidy while his wife dashed off to get tea and coffee ready in the parish room next to the church. The regulars would gather there, encouraging any visitors to join them. Father Diamond, and Father O'Connor of course when he was there, would join them too. It was nice, as Mrs. Armitage was always saying, to have a little get-together after mass. A good thing for the oldies, who might otherwise go for months without anyone to talk to other than the checkout girls in supermarkets.

Mrs. Armitage knew some of these old people well. She had been a regular at the Sacred Heart since she and Larry came to Battersea in 1972, just after they were married. Their two sons were christened there, had made their First Communions and been confirmed. It was Mrs. Armitage's hope that one or both would also be married in this church. Over the decades Mrs. Armitage had seen children born and growing up; young wives aging into widows; men who when young had stood at the back of the church during the services, if they had come at all, slowly creeping from there toward the altar as they grew older, and now hobbling painfully into the topmost pews. One of these was Mr. Kalinowski, who had been part of General Anders's army, a brave and lively man, who now, having lost his wife, his daughter, his hair, his teeth, lived on his own in a little flat and walked with difficulty, leaning on two sticks. Mrs. Armitage dropped in on him at least once a week to see if he needed anything. As she said to Larry, the easiest things get hard when you are old. She had once found Mr. Kalinowski stumbling about in an unlit kitchen because he couldn't change the lightbulb. Imagine that, he had said to Mrs. Armitage, half-laughing and half-crying. I used to fly a Spitfire, now I can't even climb up on a chair to change a bulb!

Mr. Kalinowski, Mrs. Pereira, Joan who couldn't get to church since she did her hip, Mrs. McFarlane, Phelim, Sheila, Antoinette; all friends of Mrs. Armitage, and on her visiting list. She'd keep a lookout for them on a Sunday and if they weren't there she'd make sure to pop in on them during the week, check they were okay. It was easier to do that now that she had only a part-time job at the bus depot. And it didn't take long to stick your head round a door or have a quick cup of tea.

Today, though, there was a feeling of uncertainty in the air. The mass had not been interrupted; the organist had reached the last bar of the final hymn. But, as soon as he had done so, the visitors had all converged on the chapel. Mr. and Mrs. Armitage stayed on their seats. Sorry, the chapel's closed, Mrs. Armitage said to anyone who tried to slide in past her. You can't go in there now. There were muted protests but nothing more until one young girl thrust her face close to Mrs. Armitage. Those who hide the truth will burn in hell, she hissed. Just then Father Diamond arrived. His collar and soutane, the badge of authority; even the angry girl moved back and stood aside. It's a health and safety issue, Father Diamond announced. I'm afraid that if we cannot keep people from clambering on the altar and the furniture, we will simply have to close the church. I wonder, Larry, would you kindly stay on here, until the last worshipers have left?

Meanwhile Mary-Margaret O'Reilly was still in her place at the end of a pew, kneeling, her head bowed over her crossed arms. Mrs. Armitage glanced at her. As a rule she was rather scornful of the conspicuously devout, the supplicants who knelt in front of statues with their hands clasped and their lips moving; they made her think of the Pharisees, strutting through the temple. Even so, she could hardly go and tap Mary-Margaret on her shoulder, tell her to get a move on. Somewhat reluctantly, Mrs. Armitage went off to make the coffee.

Larry Armitage stacked hymnbooks back onto their shelves and collected the discarded service sheets. There were a couple of women still peering into the chapel, another kneeling before the statue of the Sacred Heart, and Mary-Margaret, in her pew. He pushed a pew back into place as noisily as he could to show that it was time to leave. The organist clattered down from the organ loft. Just as Larry was beginning to wonder what else he could do to clear the place, Father Diamond came out of the sacristy again, locking the door behind him. Thank you, Larry, he said. I think it might be wise to close the church, for once. I'm going to turn off the lights.

This unambiguous signal served its purpose. The last stragglers headed toward the door and Mary-Margaret got to her feet. But, instead of making for the door, she edged down the length of the pew, encumbered by her shopping bag, in the direction of the chapel. Larry got there before her. It's closed, he said. But not to me, said Mary-Margaret. To everyone, said Larry. But He'll be wondering where I am, said Mary-Margaret. He might need more ointment.

Larry, who hadn't a clue what she was saying, stuck to his guns. It's closed, he said again. Health and safety. Mary-Margaret's face crumpled and she began to cry, her mouth squared like a child's. Father Diamond, seeing this, came hurrying to Larry's rescue. Now, dear, he said. What's all this? Let's go and have a cup of tea and talk about it. You and me. Together.

Mary-Margaret allowed herself to be led toward the door. Following the woman and the priest, in the unaccustomed dimness of the church, among the shrouded figures, Larry felt something stir or shift, a mere shiver, unseen and almost imperceptible. For no real reason he was reminded of the game that children play, Grandmother's footsteps, the tagged child standing poised and tense, the stalkers creeping stealthily toward him. A game in which both pursuers and pursued shared the pleasurable dread of being caught. Not being prone to flights of fancy, Larry dismissed the thought.

Father Diamond ushered him and Mary-Margaret out of the door before turning back to lock it from the outside. That's her, a voice called loudly. The woman!

A dozen or more people were standing on the small patch of ground outside the church. One was a man with a camera. Another was Kiti Mendoza. Having shared their experience last night on Facebook, she and Melinda Catapang had arranged to come back first thing today but Melinda had forgotten that she had to work a Sunday shift and Kiti had overslept. Quite a number of their Facebook friends, however, had made their way to the Sacred Heart in time for the early mass and, as they telephoned and texted, the word spread. Across South London messages flashed up: Eyes. Blood. Statues. Coverings.

During the morning Kiti had received several of these. Although none of them were entirely coherent, the ones that struck her forcefully were the ones about concealment. Several of her contacts, including her Auntie Rita, had complained that they were not allowed to see the crucifix. Some people had already gone back onto Facebook to say this too. The ripples of the story expanded inexorably, catching in their concentric rings the boyfriend of a girl who nursed with Kiti, a boy with ambitions to become a photojournalist. Kiti bumped into him on her way down Riverside Crescent, and gave him the details. It was exactly what four years in England had led her to expect: secrecy, dishonesty and double-dealing. Trying to find the truth round here? Forget it. A miracle? In this city of unbelievers they wouldn't know one if it hit them in the face.

The sight of Mary-Margaret at the front door of the church, flanked by a priest and a funny little man with a floppy gray mustache, was an unexpected godsend. The photographer focused his lens. Kiti rushed up with arms outspread and embraced Mary-Margaret. It's her, she said again, ecstatically. The one who saw it first.

It began to dawn on Father Diamond that Mary-

Margaret must have been spinning tales when she was in hospital. He remembered what she had said when he was visiting, something about wounds. At the time he had thought that she was raving. He did not now change his mind. Come on, dear, he told her firmly, pulling gently at her arm to disentangle her from the embrace of the young girl. Let's go and get that cup of tea. But Mary-Margaret would not be deflected. She recognized Kiti, of course, and was pleased to see her; even in her ordinary clothes the girl brought with her some of the atmosphere of the hospital—concerned, consoling, and efficient—that Mary-Margaret had so enjoyed. Is it true, they won't let you in? the girl asked her. Yes it is, said Mary-Margaret. He's locked the door.

Stella unlocked the front door while Rufus unpacked the car. Even when left empty only for a day or two a house is not the same as one inhabited and hers felt subdued to Stella, as if a faint melancholy had drifted through it while she was away, as gentle and as transitory as dust. There was once an occasion when, on coming home alone, she had opened the door and sensed a presence, although nothing was out of place and there was no unusual sound. It was late in June, the evening of a hot day, she had left the upstairs windows open at the rear of the house. She had looked quickly into her bedroom but there was nothing there, and in any case she had no sense of an intruder. Camilla's room was undisturbed but, when Stella switched on the light, she felt something move, or tremble. At first she could see nothing but then there was another flutter, very slight, and it came from a wooden clog, an ornament, on Camilla's desk beneath the window. As she neared it, her heart thumping, Stella saw the clog contained a bird, a swift; it must have flown in through the open window. Did it think the clog a nest, she wondered, or had it seemed the only place of safety in a bewildering world? The bird's wings were closed and it had settled halfway down the clog headfirst. It moved more violently as it heard her approach. What if it were to panic and flap wildly around, then what should Stella do? Beating its wings against the wood, it would be hurt, but loose it would be even more afraid. She realized that it must be a young bird, disorientated and unable, having landed, to take wing again by itself. It could not be abandoned on its barren nest. She went downstairs, opened the garden door, then ran back up to the little bird. It was frightening to touch it, but she scooped it up into her hands, and it was still between them. Mouse brown feathers, white beneath its chin. An infinitely tender thing. She carried it downstairs and into the twilit garden, where she opened her hands and launched it and it flew.

There was no message from her daughter in her in-box. Be sensible, Stella told herself. That doesn't mean anything's happened, it simply means she's busy. Or that she hasn't been able to get onto the Internet. Camilla's last message had mentioned trekking. Stella envisaged her daughter deep in tropical jungle, sipping rainwater from the fluted flower of some exotic plant. Night fell with no warning there, and then the dark was absolute; would Camilla know this, would she stay on the beaten path?

Idiot, said Stella sternly. At eighteen Camilla was already more experienced in some ways than Stella was herself. She had found her own way to the north of Thailand after all; she thought nothing of traveling alone. Stella, on the other hand, had never even eaten dinner in a restaurant by herself. Why was it that a woman eating on her own was somehow sad? Or, if not actually sad, she seemed so. Stella remembered a summer holiday, a beachside restaurant on the Ile de Ré. She and Rufus had been there with the children. There was a woman, English by the sound of her when she spoke in French, on her own and elegantly dressed in a pale pink linen skirt. She had ordered the fruits de mer. The plate came, hugely laden, all those shells and tentacles and claws. The woman ate methodically and with relish, cracking the crab claws, extracting the flesh of mollusks with a pin. Stella, sitting at the table next to hers, surrounded by her happy children—sand on the soles of their feet, their blond hair bleached, enjoying their Cokes and plates of frites—had tried not to stare. Poor thing, she whispered to Rufus. Nonsense, Rufus said, she's obviously having a lovely time. Those oysters look delicious. But, when the woman had finished, a clumsy waiter clearing plates had overbalanced and tipped hers right into her lap. The woman stood up with a little cry, and other waiters rushed to her, dabbing at her ineffectually with napkins while bits of shell and the juices of fish dripped all down her skirt. The apologies were profuse and the woman gracious, but what would she do now, asked Stella, would she hold her head high and walk back to her hotel through the elegant resort, stinking, stained and wet? Camilla said of course she wouldn't. She'd simply go to the nearest smart boutique and buy herself a very nice pair of trousers. But Stella couldn't shake the image from her mind. She saw the woman dressing that morning in her solitary room, choosing the pink skirt, girding herself for a restaurant lunch. She saw her slinking back, rinsing the ruined skirt, resolving to have room service for the remainder of the holiday, eating chicken sandwiches alone, off her bedside table.

Rufus came into the study, saying he needed the computer. He'd do a couple of hours' work and what would she do, was there anything worth watching on the box? Would it be all right if they had supper fairly late? He must get cracking on with the first draft of his speech.

Stella had never been entirely sure why Rufus chose to go into politics. He used to be a banker. She had asked him, of course she'd asked him, in different ways on many occasions, but his answers were not precise. The fact that an old school friend, one to whom Rufus was still close, had vaulted with apparent ease over every hurdle to become Leader of the Opposition, had much to do with Rufus's decision, Stella thought. Rufus would say he wanted a challenge, was bored with banking, had made enough money to retire on but was too young to give up working, felt he had something to contribute. Stella suspected that in fact what he relished was the sense of belonging to a powerful inner group. As an investment banker he had had power of sorts but now, with his party forecast to win the next election, he scented real influence, the power that changed lives, made history, made its possessors famous. Rufus was determined and ambitious. His friend had hoisted him onto the Shadow Cabinet as soon as he decently could. There were great things just around the corner, Rufus was sure, and Stella would support him, as she always did.

Before Rufus won his safe seat at a by-election in 2003, he had consulted Stella. Felix then was four years old, Barnaby and Camilla in their teens. This ought to be a partnership, Rufus explained. We ought to be a team. The hours are long, there's the going to and fro from Dorset. Stella, I'll need your help.

He had never asked for help before. A man armored from birth by money and privilege, he had always seemed self-sufficient, confident to a point some might consider arrogant. When Stella met him, Rufus was already a success. Stella was a young official in the Foreign Office at the time but she knew that her career stood little chance when she married Rufus. She would not be able to accept a posting overseas and, besides, she wanted children. She went on working at a London desk until Barnaby was born, relinquished it to be with him and, soon, Camilla. When both of them had started school, she returned to the department as a part-time translator. Stella's mother was Italian, from Verona; she grew up bilingual, and at university had also studied Portuguese and French. The new job suited her; she enjoyed the discipline of exact translation, choosing the correct and perfect word from the alternatives available, as a mosaic artist chooses from a tray of tesserae or a jeweler the right stone for a setting.

But Rufus wanted her to give it up. It's not as if we need the money, and I just don't see how you'll fit it in with all the new commitments and with Felix. Felix, her unexpected gift, her soul's delight. When Stella found that she was pregnant, Rufus was displeased. Two healthy children was enough, he said; to ask for more was tempting fate. And with Barney and Camilla growing up, he was looking forward to the amplitude precluded by small children. More time with her. Because she had not been planning to conceive, Stella had been taking drugs to treat an ear infection. Can you be sure the fetus won't have been affected? Rufus asked. And you are older than you were. I don't want to put any pressure on you, but . . .

Love incarnate, children were, thought Stella. She had not known what love could mean until she held her first-born in her arms. The promise of more time with the children convinced her to agree with Rufus. Now, six years later, she asked herself if she had made the right decision. Despite the endless journeying to and from the constituency, there were altogether too many hours to fill. Rufus was increasingly swept up into a world where she did not belong, or want to. Unspoken between Stella and her husband was the possibility that she did not share his opinions or his beliefs—if beliefs were what pragmatic Rufus held. Unspoken, as Rufus never asked her. And, if he had, she would not have known how to give a truthful answer. But she did feel she had a duty to her husband. Duty was so much easier to quantify than love.

Fidelma O'Reilly heard the key turn in the lock. Mary-Margaret had not spoken to her since Thursday evening and she was beginning to wonder if her daughter was ever coming back. Fidelma was used to waiting but even she had begun to think that some kind of action might have to be taken if Mary-Margaret had gone permanently missing. Also she was hungry. She had eaten all the food they had; there was nothing left but a jar of pickle. That morning, when she had finished the last slice of bread, she had briefly weighed her options. There was no one she could telephone. She never had a visitor except, on occasion, Father O'Connor, unsolicited, and the doctor. Your woman from the Social had been round a year or two ago but, assured by Mary-Margaret that everything was quite all right, she had not been back. How long would half a jar of pickle keep body and soul together? Fidelma dug a finger into the jar and scooped out a sticky cube of something brown that was both sweet and acid in her mouth.

Well, no real need to worry. Although she had never done it, Fidelma knew you could ring for a pizza. Or Chinese. Myriad leaflets saying so came floating through the letter box and fetched up in a drift on the kitchen counter until Mary-Margaret got round to throwing them away. All you had to do was call a number. But then, of course, you'd have to open the front door. You'd have to heave yourself up when you heard the doorbell; you'd have to squeeze yourself down the narrow hall. Stand there at the door and count out the money, on show for the world and his wife to see.

So the sound of Mary-Margaret's key was a relief. Fidelma stayed where she was and Mary-Margaret came in. A proper mess and all she was: brown streaks on her skirt, her hair unwashed, a clump of it all matted and a lump of it apparently cut off. Her wrist in a tight bandage. I was on the radio, she said.

You'd better get yourself cleaned up, Fidelma answered.

Oh no, this skirt's a holy relic. They nearly had it off me then and there, but I promised that I'd bring it back. It did feel funny, though, when I realized I was walking through the streets in my Savior's precious blood! But otherwise I'd only have my knickers.

Fidelma considered Mary-Margaret. She would not have had her down as an imaginative girl. Quite the opposite, indeed; she had always been distressingly attached to the plain truth. When Mary-Margaret was a little girl, Fidelma was forever having to translate for her the things that people said. "Once in a blue moon," for instance, or "He'd talk the hind legs off a donkey." When is the moon blue? her child would ask. Can a donkey stand up on three legs? It would try the patience of a saint, having to explain things to her all the time. But that was in the days when she and Mary-Margaret had still gone out a bit together; now Mary-Margaret went off on her own and made what sense she might of the outside world with no assistance from her mother.

That cut on the head must have been more serious than it looked, Fidelma thought. Odd that the hospital had let her daughter out in such a bad way, still deranged. The embers of a feeling that had not burned in Fidelma for a long time shifted a little to reveal the faintest glow. She had taken care of Mary-Margaret once, had fed her, clothed her, rocked her, sung for her the sad songs of her own childhood. She had kept her, which was much more to the point. Oh, it would have been the simplest thing to do what everybody urged her to, or ordered her to do, in fact. Back into the convent, have the wretched thing. Keep your eyes averted as they bear it off. A good Catholic couple standing by, pacing in the waiting room, desperate to be a mummy and a daddy, but needing outside help with that achievement. Never fear, the babe will want for nothing, these decent folk will love it as if it were their own.

It happened all the time, Fidelma knew. The trick, she had been told, was not to see the wean at all. Close your eyes when it comes out, don't ask if it's a boy or girl, don't give it a second thought. There's something you can take to dry the milk up, when it comes, although it has to be admitted that your chest will fairly ache. But putting the baby to the breast, even for a few days, now that's a terrible mistake. If you do that you're lost forever, girl. When they take the child away, you'll grieve for life.

Fidelma had kept her eyes wide open the whole time. She had learned to do that when she was not much older than a babe herself. Let your guard down even for a minute and you'd be very sorry; there'd be some old devil of a priest coming at you with his poking fingers and his pink tongue lolling out. Or a sister finding fault with you, when you'd done no wrong. Woe betide the child who closed her eyes to danger. She'd find herself locked up in the thick blackness of the cellar or locked out in the coldness of the night.

Come now, Mary-Meg, Fidelma said. Did you get to the shops? Good girl, why don't I make you something while you go and have a nice hot bath?

It was not a major story but nonetheless it was still news. Tucked away in the middle of the tabloids and on local radio: eyes open, statue bleeds. Pretty Kiti Mendoza was there, in a photograph taken outside the church, looking sweet and pious. So was Father Diamond, clutching the great key of the church defensively in his hand. Cover-up.

Authorities have ordered the figure of Jesus to be wrapped up in a curtain and are banning visitors. Barring access to the church. Why? What are they frightened of?

Hints of a conspiracy by Roman Catholic priests—always an attractive target—gave the story resonance and it spread as fast as an enormous oil slick. Speculation about earlier attempts to cover up the truth—of the marriage of Jesus to Mary Magdalene, for instance, or the whereabouts of Jesus' body—was a diverting way to fill the hollow miles of space. By Monday evening the crowd outside the church was large.

Father Diamond consulted the diocesan office. The Secretary to the Bishop reminded him of policy: outbreaks of hysteria are to be discouraged. They are not healthy and do not give glory to God. The face of Our Lady on a pizza, Our Lord on a slice of toast! Such a load of hocus-pocus, with no place at all in the contemporary world. The very last thing we need, given all the trials we face today—have you seen the news from Ireland?—is a bunch of hostile journalists accusing us of being stuck in a medieval time warp and fanning superstition. Ammunition to the Angry Anarchists Brigade! They'd have a field day.

This isn't quite the same as a slice of toast, Father Diamond said, scrupulously. No, the secretary agreed. But as you and I know perfectly well, plaster figurines don't bleed. Nor do they open their eyes. They don't have eyes. They have molded eyelids and a dab of paint.

Some of them have glass eyes, Father Diamond pointed out. And eyelashes made of real hair. But both men knew that was beside the point. The question remained, though, of how to pacify the crowds. People keep arriving, Father

Diamond told the secretary. Bringing flowers and cards. Their intentions on scraps of paper. They want to get into the church.

Let them in, the secretary said. At certain times. When you can be there too. Put a notice on the door announcing when the church is open. Put another in the chapel explaining why the cross is veiled and when the veil will be removed. You might be in for a nice surprise on Easter Sunday!

All right, said Father Diamond. There was nothing else to do. If only Father O'Connor were around, but there was almost another month of his sabbatical to go. Father Diamond asked for a grant toward the cost of security, as it seemed to him he might need some guards. Some members of the crowd could be positively hostile.

Mrs. Armitage, with her dog Tommy, ran into Stella, who was on her way to the park, on Wednesday afternoon. They stopped to talk. What a carry-on, Mrs. Armitage said. All that stuff and nonsense at the church. Yes, said Stella. I saw there were a lot of people. What's been going on? Oh, said Mrs. Armitage, you've been away, of course. I forget that you are not around much on a Sunday. That poor fool of a woman, Mary-Margaret O'Reilly—remember the cut on the head and so forth—well, it seems that she's been going round and saying that she saw the cross in the Chapel of the Holy Souls—you know the one, the crucifix—she saw it shedding blood. Or something. Something about it opening its eyes. Anyway, she told them in the hospital and word spread on the grapevine and next thing we know there's a mob of hysterical women trying to see the crucifix for themselves. But, of course, it's covered. So cue a great outcry about unholy goings-on and hostile clergy hushing the whole thing up. Poor Father D. It's all a bit over his head, I think. But things are quieter today. He's had to close the church between services but there's a big notice saying so, and people seem to have accepted that. Or maybe it's just been a nine-day wonder. Or a three-day one, more like.

Do you think Mary-Margaret really did see something? Stella asked.

Of course not, Mrs. Armitage laughed. God doesn't need a calling card, for goodness sake. Didn't Jesus say the blessed are those who do not see and yet believe? I can't be doing with bones and blood and magic shenanigans; a load of mumbo jumbo this stuff is, in my opinion. Miracles are one thing—who's to say—I mean we all know the Lord moves in mysterious ways—but bleeding statues? Never!

I'm sure you're right, said Stella. Anyway. Tell me—how's Fraser? He should be back quite soon?

Three weeks. We're counting the days, as you'd expect. He's not bad at writing, I'll give him that, but he doesn't always get the time and he has to save his phone calls up for Steph. Well. No news is good news, I always say.

Yes, of course. I do feel for you.

Thank you, dear, said Mrs. Armitage, rather annoyed that her eyes had filled, unaccountably, with tears. You'll keep him in your prayers, won't you.

Stella hugged the older woman briefly and they went their separate ways. It was a cold day, blustery, and Stella pulled her coat more tightly round her as she walked. The park was almost deserted at that hour of the day; a solitary runner, old men and women walking dogs. Cherry blossom blown off branches by the wind, skittering in the air like flakes of snow; crocuses, and daffodils. Daffydowndilly, Lenten lily, she said the names out loud. There was a time when the flowers of the field took their place in the church's seasons too. Snowdrops, Mary's tapers for the Feast of Candlemas, pasqueflowers for Passiontide. The holly and the ivy; berries, glistening drops of red. Stella remembered Mary-Margaret O'Reilly's blood and shivered. It was a pity that these connections were now all but lost. The poetry there must have been, that rhymed customs and calendars, feast days and old beliefs, flowers, magic, miracles and spells. Oak and ash and thorn. Gone now except for feeble echoes: Christmas wreaths and mistletoe, harvest festival displays festooned with cans and packets. In Italy chrysanthemums are the flowers of the dead. Grave goods in gold and bronze, and asphodel their food. How can Mrs. Armitage bear it? Stella asked herself. To be always in the brace position, to stop her eyes and ears to the daily news?

In England there are flowers for the dead by waysides, tied to railings, wilting in cellophane. Sad bunches of carnations such as are on sale in the forecourts of petrol stations, where the bereaved must go to find them. Isn't it a bit of a pain doing the flowers in church? Rufus had asked her. It's the sort of thing that women do when they haven't anything more important to occupy their time. Not women like you, that is.

It doesn't take that long, Stella had answered vaguely. How could she explain? She, who seldom attended any service, who abided by the faith of her upbringing more by default than through conscious option, who might say in prayer: help Thou my unbelief. Well, the flowers were a small service that gave pleasure in the doing. Stella loved the essential balancing, the silky feel of petals, the scent of lilies, sweet peas, roses.

Father Diamond, also walking in the park that afternoon, also looking for escape, saw the flurries of white blossom and thought of Santa Maria Maggiore, built on the summit of the Esquiline Hill to a plan forecast by the Virgin, in an August fall of snow. That was a true miracle, in the summer heat of Rome. Imagine the cold crystals on the sunbaked ground, frost tips on the yellowed blades of grass. Every year on the anniversary of the snowfall, the fifth of August, a trapdoor in the ceiling of the great basilica is opened and a shower of white rose petals floats down onto the nave. Santa Maria della Neve, Our Lady of the Snows.

Mary-Margaret was disappointed. It had been fun talking to the man from the newspaper and the radio girl with a gold stud in her tongue. Actually, it was hard to concentrate on the questions the girl asked, so mesmerizing was the shiny nugget flashing in and out as she opened and closed her mouth. Mary-Margaret shuddered to think how much it must have hurt, that piercing. But for some reason, the little nurse had stolen all the limelight since. Which was just not fair. It was not to her that the Lord had made Himself known in the beginning. But there she was, chattering on and on about the way He had opened His eyes and looked straight at her; she could see His eyes glowing in the dark. Still, Mary-Margaret consoled herself, the truth would soon be out. She was the chosen one, the handmaid of the Lord. She just needed a quiet moment on her own with Him so He could tell her what to do next. Meanwhile she supposed she had to keep going with the everyday stuff of life, but that was hard after you'd been chosen. Shopping, cooking, tidying up—these things seemed quite trivial, really, in comparison with the task Our Lord might have in mind. There was no doubt that she was marked out for something special; but having to wait around for it was getting Mary-Margaret down.

So it was luck that put her in the way of Mrs. Abdi, on Wednesday afternoon. Mrs. Abdi was waiting for the lift and as usual was burdened by plastic bags and children; there was a baby in a buggy who was even littler than Shamso. She looked anxious, her face was strained beneath her veil. Mrs. Abdi's English wasn't up to much, but they rubbed along. Baby sick, she said. Doctor. Small children no got school. Oh I see, said Mary-Margaret. So you've got to cart the whole lot with you to the doctor's? Well don't go doing that. I'll look after them, at your place, if you like. Mrs. Abdi seemed grateful and relieved.

And pure joy for Mary-Margaret. Sagal, Samatar, Bahdoon, Shamso; the older two still at school. Shamso cried when his mother left him, but his sister cheered him up and Mary-Margaret made him happier still with a game of hide-and-seek behind the living room curtain. She wrapped it round her so she seemed to disappear, then popped out saying boo, and each time Shamso screamed in wild delight. He must think I've truly vanished, Mary-Margaret realized.

After a while Shamso showed signs of getting tired. Mary-Margaret poured Coke into a bottle for him and into beakers for the others. She rummaged about and found some packets of crisps. Mrs. Abdi's cupboards smelled different and delicious, smells that Mary-Margaret could not identify, foreign herbs and spices. Hyssop and aloes, she said to herself. Hyssop and bitter aloes.

She lined up the children on the sofa in front of the television and sat herself down too. They watched quietly, once they'd eaten their crisps. Shamso suddenly fell asleep, the bottle plopping wetly from his mouth. He was on Mary-Margaret's bad side, the side of the injured wrist, so she reached over and hoisted him onto her lap, where he could rest more easily. He did not wake. She cradled him gently in the curve of her arm, his head was heavy on her breast. She buried her face in his corkscrew curls; he smelled of cereal and Twiglets and something sugary—she thought of brightly colored boiled sweets. Mary-Margaret kissed him lightly. This child sleeping trustfully on her, the warm and solid weight of him, his sticky mouth, his minute sneakers, made her so happy that it felt like heartache.

Felix Morrison drew a cross through Wednesday on his chart. Seven more days to go. The week would creep on as slowly as an injured tortoise, Felix knew, but at least it *would* creep on, and then his mother would be there to take him home. From where he was at present, in the form room, it was hard to picture home. He could visualize his bedroom, the garden, or the kitchen, but he couldn't *feel* them, or feel what it would be like to be inside them, with their particular textures and scents. And yet, oddly, when he was at home, he could summon up the experience of school quite easily. He had only to open his school trunk, to breathe in its blue and gray interior the mingled smells of fish and cold and ink and people, fear and polish, disinfectant, gym mats, wet socks and muddy boots that were the essence of his school. A thing he noticed was that nowhere in the school was there a trace of softness. It was a place of angles, corners, unforgiving surfaces; concrete stairs, unheated corridors, Astroturf, the sharp edges of metal beds.

Softness must be girlie, Felix thought. Home was soft. His sister's pink bedroom, his pile of cuddly toys, carpets, the flowers his mother put in every room. His mother was soft. He pushed her from his mind, hunched himself up on his chair like a vigilant bird and licked his knee to have the tang of it, his bruised knee bone. Any minute now the bell would go, and his prep was still undone. *Columbas deis sacrificant*, he wrote. They sacrifice doves to the gods.

Have you heard from Fraser? Father Diamond asked Mrs. Armitage, after mass on Thursday morning, when she was beginning the weekly clean. Indirectly, as it were, she said. Steph read us out the letter that came for her yesterday. He didn't say a lot, mind, except that he's looking forward to getting home. The lads put on such brave faces, don't they, but it takes its toll, the time out there.

I'm sure it does, said Father Diamond; he is always in my thoughts.

And it was true, almost. If not Fraser himself, whom Father Diamond hardly knew since he was not a churchgoer like his parents, then all the others, the fresh-faced young men in desert camouflage, for whom Fraser was a symbol. Every single day brought news of them. But not news that could be welcomed. One after the other they appeared, relegated by now to news in brief; ordinary-looking, smiling boys under their regimental berets. Or in coffins, covered with the Union Jack. Sometimes the reports included testimonials by commanding officers or the words of wives or girlfriends left behind. How were these sad words made known? Father Diamond often wondered. Did reporters go round to the homes of the deceased and solemnly set down their threadbare, heartbreaking epitaphs: born a legend, died a hero, the best son in the world?

At a railway station a few months before, Father Diamond had come across a group of these young men, transacting with a ticket seller. In uniform, with kit bags, their names sewn on and on their shoulder flashes the letters ISAF. Among the other would-be travelers in their unremarkable clothes these dappled boys stood out like young stags in a concrete wasteland, eagles in a nest of doves. Father Diamond felt a peculiar need to touch one, to tug a thread from a uniform and keep it safely, to write their names down in his notebook, to hold on to something of them before they began their journey to the other world. It was morbid, he knew, to fear that they would never use the return halves of their railway warrants and yet he did fear that as, he supposed, onlookers had feared that Theseus would not make his way back from the monster at the center of the maze.

Boys dream of being heroes and when he was a boy, Father Diamond dreamed too. In his teens, more realistically, he resolved to be a professor of mathematics. As such he would possess a permanent license to explore the marvelous world of symmetry, proportion, symbol, ratio, equilibrium; a world that appeared to him as a series of interlocking rooms carved out of pristine whiteness. But at university, in the Faculty of Mathematics, he began to see that he was not in fact the author of his life. He fought that realization, at the start. He got his first and then his master's; he gained his doctorate. Cambridge offered him a lectureship. And then, helpless, he gave in to the pressure that had been growing inside him like a teratoma and embarked on the gradual process of becoming a priest.

It is usual to talk of a vocation to the priesthood. Father Diamond experienced something that was more like a violent shove than a gentle call. He was like a man walking along a cliff-top path who thinks he knows where he is going but is constantly blown off course by an enormously strong wind. After a while, it was too exhausting to resist. And dangerous as well. If he did not let the wind take him where it willed, it might blow him off the edge onto sharp rocks. He had to accept that his chosen destination was a mirage; the oasis was somewhere else.

This was not a thing of which Father Diamond could speak. He did not understand it yet himself. One day, he hoped, that irresistible force would make its purpose clear to him but so far it had not, and the oasis was still a long way out of sight. In the meantime Father Diamond stumbled on, head down, collar turned against the rain.

As a novice he had thought of missionary work. There were heroes in that field, to be sure. Priests who risked persecution, illness, even imprisonment, to be porters of the word of God. Within his own order, men had been taken hostage by militants or killed on official command for championing the poor and the oppressed. His superiors, however, had other plans for him. As a solitary spirit with a tendency to arrogance he had to have his sharp edges buffed appropriately smooth. What better mill to grind him in than an inner-city parish?

Even so, after a decade and more, Father Diamond could still find himself yearning for a different plot, another route, an unanticipated ending to his story. Those warriors in their clumping boots and separateness stopped him in his tracks. I should be there too, he thought. Shoulder to shoulder with these men whose forced obedience to a higher power was not unlike his own.

The church was quiet today. Only Mrs. Armitage and the other regular parishioners had been at mass, and there was no sign of the crowds of earlier that week. All the crosses and the statues were correctly veiled; things were back in their rightful order and Mrs. Armitage's mop swished soothingly across the floor, leaving the odor of red polish in its wake. It seems to have calmed down, Father Diamond remarked to her.

I told you it would be a three-day wonder, she replied.

Did you actually have a look at the crucifix last week? he asked. After Mary-Margaret's fall?

No I didn't. Not that I recall. It was a bit of a panic, wasn't it, with her bleeding head and all. I do remember making sure that everything was tidy. But I didn't specifically check the cross because I could see that there was nothing wrong with it. Should I have done? Why?

No, no, he said, hastily. I was just wondering. That's all.

Mary-Margaret came in just then, through the main door, holding a feather duster. Mrs. Armitage stopped polishing and looked at her doubtfully. Should you be here? she asked.

Why not? said Mary-Margaret. My head is better. I had the stitches out, that's why I'm a bit late this morning. And I only need one arm to dust.

That's good, dear, said Father Diamond. Good of you to come. We do appreciate it, don't we, Mrs. Armitage? But please don't go climbing up on any chairs now, will you? We don't want another drama!

Mary-Margaret laughed. Nee-naw, nee-naw, she said, and scuttled off to dust the pulpit. Like a demented hen, Father Diamond thought, watching her shake russet feathers back and forth. He apologized in silence for the thought.

As far as she could see, Mary-Margaret was doing nothing untoward, but Mrs. Armitage resolved to keep a firm eye on her. She finished the floor, and Mary-Margaret dusted down the pews. The usual routine was for her to polish the altar rails with Brasso while Mary-Margaret gouged candle wax from the stands. Then they would have a cup of coffee in the sacristy with Father Diamond, if he was still about. But this morning Mary-Margaret was in a rush. She had to get to the shops and make lunch for her mother before two, when she had promised Mrs. Abdi she would look after Shamso. The little pet had taken quite a shine to her. When Mrs. Abdi got back yesterday to a scene of calm and the tot sleeping, she had been so pleased that she scrabbled around in her purse and found a fiver, which she tried to give Mary-Margaret. Mary-Margaret waved it aside. My pleasure, she told Mrs. Abdi. I'll come round again, if you like.

When Mrs. Armitage went round the back to empty the bins, Mary-Margaret nipped into the Chapel of the Holy Souls. Hello, she said. It's me, O Lord. I'm back.

There was no audible response but she had not really expected one. How was He supposed to speak, all muffled up as He was, poor thing, in that nasty cloak of purple? Yet He would know that she was there. She pictured Him, beneath His shroud, His beautiful clean body. Closing her eyes, she saw Him inclining toward her from the cross, pulling one hand free to bend down and stroke her hair. She felt His hand, gentle against her scar, tender in spite of His own grievous pain. He pushed the hair softly from her face. She seized the hand and pressed it to her lips. Her mouth against His skin, against His tightened sinews.

Mary-Margaret fell to her knees. Dearest, she said softly. Please don't think you are forsaken. I'll be back, I promise. The rocks may melt and the seas may burn if I do not . . .

What do you think you're doing? Mrs. Armitage demanded. You know this chapel is out-of-bounds. Mary-Margaret started, awkwardly turned round. Mrs. Armitage saw that there were tears streaming down her face. Come on, lass, she said, more kindly. Be a love and put the kettle on while I put away the mop.

Mary-Margaret went meekly. There was no one in the sacristy. She filled the kettle at the sink. Above the sink was a wooden panel with a row of key hooks, each one labeled in Father Diamond's meticulous handwriting. Fuse box. Garage. Sacristy. Organ. Shed. There were two sets of keys on the sacristy hook. Mary-Margaret took one and put it in the pocket of her fleece.

*

Stella stroked a velvet bud. Most of the buds had already opened to release their star-shaped flowers; the tree was heavy with them, and their fleeting scent. *Magnolia stellata.* Rufus had given it to her as a sapling when they bought this house. Wherever we live we'll have one, he had said; this plant that has your name. Other flowers were beginning to hatch in the fresh sunlight: primroses, anemones, the early clematis. Tomorrow her son Barnaby would come back from his field trip; in exactly one week's time it would be Felix's end of term. Why had she consented to send Felix to boarding school? She thought of Mrs. Armitage; her son in such danger, and so far away.

Would her sense of being incomplete without her children lessen when all three were fully grown? People had told her she was fortunate, when Felix went away. It's like a second honeymoon, a friend had said. You fall in love with your husband all over again when you have more time to spend with him, time alone together.

A robin sang a scolding song from his sentry post in a trailing branch of ivy. Stella laughed. Are you telling me it's time I went inside and left you in peace to feed the brood? she asked the bird. You're right. She rubbed a strand of rosemary between her fingers for the scent of it on her way in. Cock Robin, with a nest of gaping beaks. The memory came to her of babies at the breast, their tiny, frantic mouths when newly born and panicking lest they be left to starve. It took weeks until they found the confidence to wait even for a minute in the expectation that, having been fed before, they were likely to be fed again. Before that the least delay caused them to cry as if their hearts would break and break again in the lonely desolation of their hunger.

Later, when they were a few months old, the babies learned the pleasures of anticipation and of gratified demand. Each, though, kept their individual style. Barnaby was leisurely, would break off to have a look around, to pat the obliging breast with his small paw, would twinkle up at Stella in mid-gulp as if he shared a wordless joke. Felix dedicated more care to the process. Women in the main tend to stay silent on the pleasure of the slow letdown, the soft pink gums, the sense of power and purpose as the sated infant falls asleep all of a sudden at the breast.

In the kitchen, Stella looked at her watch and saw with a jolt that her guests would be arriving in two hours. She was giving a supper party, one of a series, to be held each Thursday during this parliamentary session. It was a scheme of Rufus's. He wanted to create a contemporary model of the "At Homes" of the thirties, when society hostesses gathered thinkers and politicians in their drawing rooms, creating a stage on which the brilliant could shine and afterward record their bons mots in their diaries. Realizing that no one nowadays would know how to respond to an At Home invitation or rise to the occasion of a salon, Rufus had decided that the modern equivalent was the kitchen supper. Every week he and Stella would invite a mixture of old friends, the more attractive neighbors, political colleagues, journalists and anyone else who had influence, was likely to be flattered, and would respond to Rufus. Kitchen sups, he told them all. Spag bol. No need for your best bib and tucker.

This evening Stella was cooking a fish stew. She had already pared the peel from an orange and left it to dry slowly on the Aga. Now she began to work out the time it would take to complete her preparations. She should have begun them earlier; she would have to rush, there was no time left to wash her hair.

She shook mussels from the bowl in which they had been resting into a basinful of water. They imparted a faint breath of the sea. Some clamped their shells more tightly shut when they felt the impact, one or two gave up the ghost and sagged forlornly open. Stella remembered Felix's mingled horror and amazement when he discovered mussels were alive. Alive even when you cook them? he had asked. Well, yes, but only for a minute or two, she'd said. That's so mean; you ought to kill them properly first. That night she had found a mussel sequestered in a mug of water by his bed. She knew that Felix would have given it a name.

Such beautiful things, she thought, these mussels. Their sleek shells gleaming in the water, pearl-tinged at the hinges, a darkness that was full of color—green and gray and bronze. It was their ordinariness that put them beyond remark. As with many other things—the iridescent feathers on a drake's neck in the winter, so startling a green; the buds of a magnolia; the high polish of a newly released conker—the mussels were too familiar to be a real cause of wonder. We look out for the rare and the exotic. The magnificence of a peacock's tail, the flash of diamonds in a seam of coal. And yet what could be more exotic than a cock pheasant in a field of frozen turnips on a winter morning, his ruby markings and his emerald green head?

Beautiful though they might be, it was hard work to clean these mussels. She scraped away their cargo of barnacles, her fingers cold and swollen. There was still squid to clean, fennel to chop, and garlic. She must lay the table, fetch ironed napkins from the linen cupboard, find fresh candles, make aioli, and whip cream for the apple tart.

Rufus got home just before the guests arrived at eight o'clock. Did you put the Prosecco in the fridge? he asked. Good girl. I'll go and shave.

Stella pinned up her unwashed hair with a silver clip and hoped it would pass muster. In the bathroom mirror she saw a stranger's face, older than her own, with sadness in the eyes. Get a grip, she said out loud, and brushed on a quick coat of mascara.

A beautiful woman, Rufus thought, but did not have time to say. Azin Qureshi thought so too, when Stella opened the door to him and his wife. He had not met her or Rufus before; his wife, an editor at *The Economist*, was the intended guest, and he had only been invited for the sake of politeness. He noticed the tendrils of hair, the fine bones of her face. With a professional eye he noted too the signs of tension round her mouth.

Sparkling wine beside the fire in the drawing room; the kitchen table laid with silver, lit by candles. Rufus beamed around the table at his guests. They had come downstairs to a kitchen warm with the scents of garlic and tomatoes; they were comforted by Stella's game terrine and Rufus's fine claret. Between the fish stew and the apple tart, Stella served a perfectly ripe Roquefort and conversation flowed. It centered for the most part on the dire financial state the country had suddenly found itself in, apparently to everyone's complete surprise. We are on the edge of a cliff, a banker said. And the trouble is that no one knows how far we'll have to fall.

Stella listened to the chatter with half her mind on refilling glasses, clearing plates, offering more food. She understood, of course, that the economic situation was important, but she had heard an identical conversation the previous Thursday, and the week before. No one particularly sought her opinion; she was left to produce dinner and consider the assorted guests. The banker; the Shadow Secretary of State for Children, Schools and Families, with her partner; a headhunter; Jenny McCann from *The Economist* and Azin Qureshi, her husband, who was sitting on Stella's left. He was a community psychiatrist at St. Elizabeth's. From time to time the others solicited his views on the effect of the crisis on mental-health care or the Health Service more generally but, like Stella, he did not have much to offer the debate. Instead, like her, he listened.

By the time the tart was eaten the guests were too full of wine and food and too sleepy to talk facts, but too settled to leave the table and go home. As usual the evening trailed away into inconsequential talk—of Easter holidays, the likelihood of snow on ski slopes at this time of the year, Easter eggs and how it was just a matter of time before someone marketed a chocolate calendar for Lent. Speaking of which, the headhunter, who was also a neighbor, said: did anyone see the story about the church at the end of this street?

The woman recounted the story, in a slightly altered version. Stella knows the church, said Rufus vaguely.

There's such a lot of this sort of nonsense, the Shadow Minister's partner said. You know. Jesus on a burger, Allah on a piece of aubergine. Sorry, he said then, in the direction of Azin Qureshi. Azin laughed.

But, the headhunter interjected, who's to say it's non-sense? Really? I mean, okay, the burger is a bit far-fetched but, you know, seeing things, like visions . . .

"The vision thing," the banker quoted. But these days, if someone said they'd seen a vision, you'd lock them up in safe surroundings. I mean securely padded ones, wouldn't you, Azin?

I don't know about locking them up, Azin said, but I expect that if their visions were troublesome to them, we'd consider medication. A lot of borderline psychotics "see" things or hear voices.

Wasn't that the thing with saints? asked Jenny. They were actually epileptics? Or whatever. Basically, in need of medication. All that falling around in fits and going into ecstasies and developing those marks on their hands and feet; what are they called, I can't remember?

Stigmata, Stella said.

I don't actually see why it's so improbable, the head-hunter went on. Voices and visions, I mean. As a society, we're curiously selective about what we choose to believe. Or allow other people to believe, perhaps. Yet millions of people do believe that God gave Moses ten command-ments, or that Allah dictated the Koran to Mohammed.

So much easier for him if they'd invented Dictaphones, murmured the minister.

Yes. But you have to draw a line somewhere, her partner said. What about *The Book of Mormon*? Lots of people seri-ously believe that wotsisname found the word of God bur-ied by an angel in the mud somewhere, but we know that's barking mad. So what's the difference between *The Book of Mormon* and Moses' stone tablets? Or the Koran, if it comes to that? If you ask me, a woman who thinks she saw a statue bleed falls under the same category, self-delusion.

There are more things in heaven and earth, Horatio, than are dreamt of in your philosophy, the headhunter remarked, conclusively.

That's right, said Jenny. When in doubt we turn to Shakespeare. So much safer than the Koran or the Bible.

Rufus laughed. We don't do God, he said.

Fidelma surveyed the black baby Mary-Margaret had lugged in. He was small and sticky and dressed in what Fidelma took to be pajamas, the top and bottoms printed with blue penguins. The baby looked at Fidelma and began to cry.

I hope you're getting paid to look after him, she said.

I am not, said Mary-Margaret. I'm doing it for love. And besides, if I take money it messes with my benefits. Look, Ma, look at his dinky little feet. She took a raspberry Viennese biscuit from the packet on the table and popped it into Shamso's mouth. The crying stopped.

He did indeed have tiny feet, Fidelma thought. Well, babies do, she felt like saying to her daughter. But then it was quite possibly true that Mary-Margaret had not had much to do with babies, unlike Fidelma. Eight of them there'd been, double the number of the children of Lir, with Fidelma the second eldest of the team. For a while it seemed you'd only pop out for a walk to find when you got home there was some new brat bawling its wee mouth off in the crib. There was nothing Fidelma did not know about the care and handling of babies. Even now she could bring back the smell and taste of that gripe water—Woodward's, wasn't that the name?—she used to take a nip out of the bottle for herself when her mother's back was turned.

Runny noses, cold bare feet, the saggy droop of sodden nappies. All those open mouths and empty bellies. And then there came a time when the empty bellies could no longer be half-filled, and their daddy gone. But in between there were some good times in the old place on the strand. More and more, as the years went on, those early days of childhood would return, and feel more real to Fidelma than the times she found herself adrift in now. In this slow procession of days, each one as like to the one before as to make no difference except whether she would have a feed of haddock or of bacon, what was there to dwell on but the past? And better far to go back to the old days than to admit the cold thought of the years to come.

Mary-Margaret was down on her knees with Shamso on the floor. Like a great big child herself, her mother thought. Well, of course she *was* a child in most respects, notwithstanding her thirty-three years upon this earth. This fact was not a fact on which Fidelma usually allowed herself to dwell. Today, for no reason she could name, it hit her with great force and made her softer than she should be. Play pat-a-cake with him, she said.

What's pat-a-cake? her daughter asked.

Oh you know, Mary-Meg. Reach over and I'll show you, then you can show the wean.

Mary-Margaret shuffled closer, on her knees. She put her hands up to her mother's. Her fingers were thicker than Fidelma's, despite Fidelma's size; the skin of them red and roughened, but the tips peculiarly smooth, as if washing had rubbed away the whorls. The bandage round her wrist was getting dirty. Fidelma clapped her hands together first and then gently against her daughter's. Pat-a-cake, pat-a-cake, baker's man. Bake me a cake as fast as you can . . .

Shamso laughed at the sight and sound of the women clapping. Never have I heard that before, said Mary-Margaret.

Liar, said her mother, with a stab of guilt. It could be true, of course. When Mary-Margaret was a baby, life was far too hard for games. To keep a roof over the child's head and put food into her mouth was about as much as Fidelma could ever do. Or more, from time to time. No one could expect her to play at patting too. Although, it must be said, her own mammy had somehow managed it, even with all those other mouths to fill. How else would Fidelma know the actions and the words? Perhaps it had been easier for her, because there were so many. She had only to teach the firstborn and he could pass it to the next like an inheritance, or a birthright, or a spell. Here comes a candle to light you to bed, here comes a chopper to chop off your head. How many miles to Babylon? Three-score miles and ten. Can I get there by candlelight? Yes, and back again.

Back again the words came, from the buried horde. Mary-Margaret showed Shamso. He understood the patting but not the alternating hands; in any case he chuckled, and Fidelma saw his perfect teeth, his contagious, gummy smile.

There were songs too, that her mother sang. And those she *had* sung, in her turn, to Mary-Margaret; sad songs for the most part but when you came to think of it, was there any other kind of song that would be worth the singing? Even the songs you would suppose were intended to be funny were melancholy really when you looked deep down. In Dublin's fair city, where the girls are so pretty, I first set my eyes on sweet Molly Malone. Now her ghost wheels her barrow through the streets broad and narrow, crying . . .

Crying. Fidelma's mother sang sad songs to lull her babes to sleep. All the small girls in one bed, Fidelma too, nestled warm and wriggling like a basketful of puppies. Fidelma's little sisters: Bridget, Maeve and Mary, Deirdre and Siobhan. Twelve kicking feet and twelve poking hands and somewhere in the room their mammy, sitting in the darkness, singing her sad songs. Oh mother, oh mother go dig my grave. Make it both long and narrow. Sweet William died on yester eve, and I will die tomorrow.

Fidelma might not have played with Mary-Margaret, nor read to her, nor even maybe talked, but she had sung, and that she did remember. She had sung those lullabies at night to banish darkness and will the light to come, to fill the silence which would not be filled by any spoken words within her power. And Mary-Margaret, her fat and pink and unlooked-for baby, had cooed and gurgled and tried to woo her mother into love. She had never been much trouble in herself, that at least Fidelma must admit. A placid, peaceful baby with a great capacity for sleep. Truth be told, the lullabies were never needful. As long as she was reasonably warm and reasonably fed, Mary-Margaret would fall asleep and sleep for hours, the sleep of the dead, while her solitary mother sang sad songs in the nighttime to herself.

Until she, along with Bridget, Maeve and Mary, was sentenced to the sisters, Fidelma had never heard of silence. In the cottage by the strand there were always voices. Even in the night there were children murmuring in sleep or breathing so loudly their breath itself was like a song. A memory of early on was lying in bed in the damp tangle of her sisters, wide awake and listening to the voices of her parents. Wordless voices like two lines of music, a higher and a lower, twining themselves around each other like stems of briar rose, questioning and answering, turn and turn about, a prayer and a response.

And if there had not been voices, there would have been the wind. There, on the shoreline, the wind was never still. All through each day and every night it whispered, it confided or it howled. It prowled round and round the house, looking for the cracks in windows and the bare patches in the thatch. Its banshee music rose and fell, rose and fell, was so soft sometimes that you could half forget it until it screeched again as a sharp reminder. It never relaxed its vigilance; in kindly mood it stroked the hair back off your face, in cruel it pulled it sharply.

And underneath the wind's voice was the sea's. Suck and sigh, or thunder roaring, constant as the beat of blood. Fidelma never listened to the sea, as she never listened to her heart, but once removed inland to the sisters, she listened to its absence, and the silence that replaced it was menacing and cold.

There would be seals on the rocks a few yards from the strand and once in a blue moon they would add their singing voices to the wind's and to the sea's. As children, Fidelma and the others had wanted to believe the tales of seals and mermaids, of beautiful young girls who arrived mysteriously, wived fishermen and bore them children, only to disappear as suddenly as they had come. Or seal princes who took human form and stole the hearts of lonely maidens and stole too the babes they fathered on them. In the darkness of winter nights it had been Fidelma's fearful pleasure to imagine her own mother in the other room, sliding out of bed, casting off her nightgown, slipping naked through the house, white as bone, as moonlight, white as broken shell, lifting the latch of the kitchen door, as quiet as a fish so as not to wake her trusting husband. Running down the silver sand on white feet, into the caressing sea. Finding there, in the kingdom of the drowned, the children she had pined for and forgetting the ones she'd left behind.

When Fidelma's father upped and went, she was too grown-up to think that he had gone back to the sea. But the old fears seeped into her dreams. One night she woke in terror, darting up to make sure that the youngest, Ronan, was where he should be, in his crib, not appropriated by his father and carried down to the dark depths of the cold salt sea. No trace of him for consolation but a snippet of black hair, a frond of coral and a single gold coin left as nurse's payment.

Ronan was barely three months old when he lost his father. A beautiful baby he had been, big brown eyes and dark eyelashes; maybe that explained her dreams. Fidelma had not seen her brother these forty years or more; he might as well have drowned for all she knew. And it shall come to pass on a summer's day, when the sun shines bright on every stane, I'll come and fetch my little young son, and teach him how to swim the faem.

This new pet of Mary-Margaret's had shiny dark eyes too. She was hoicking him around with her, dancing flat-footed through the rooms, trying to keep him happy. He needs some toys, she said. But we haven't any, have we? What can he play with, do you think?

Give him here, Fidelma said. Mary-Margaret dropped the child onto her lap. He sank into its depths and for a second looked as if he were about to cry again but then he settled, softly cushioned in her folds. How strange it was, Fidelma thought, to hold a child again. Hush now, she said to Shamso. There's a good boy. And she sang.

In the delight of having Barnaby back from Ethiopia, Stella forgot the previous evening and the shame of staying silent. "What would St. Peter say?" she heard the cloister voices ask—the defending of one's faith was every Christian's duty. But Stella's own was pale, she felt, flimsy as the roots of wild violets and as like to shrivel in harsh light. And anyway, her own table was not the proper place for declaration, if it might discomfort the invited guests. She turned her attention to her eldest child, this amazing person who had a man's full height but not yet a man's full breadth; who was impossibly narrow, filthy, travel-stained and beautiful, casually pleased to see her, eager to be off again with friends almost as soon as he was home. He dropped his backpack in the hall. His sandaled feet were dark with dust and he had grown a beard. When Stella reached to touch it he shied away. In his bag he had a present for her, a small wooden figure, cracked and worn but still recognizably the figure of an angel, one wing missing, the other broken to a stub. I bought it in the market, Barney said. The man swore that it was very old but you can't really tell. Anyway, I thought you'd like it.

I do, she said. It's beautiful. Thank you so much, darling. Would you like a bath?

Barney was to stay two nights in London before leaving for Shropshire, where his girlfriend lived. Stella and Rufus were to drive down then to the constituency, where she would remain until Thursday, Felix's end of term. Rufus had marked off a whole day in his diary for time alone with Stella. Afterward he was going to New York. The family would gather again in London on Easter Sunday, when Stella's mother and stepfather would join them, with Rufus's brothers and their wives. Two branches of a family entwined, a day of feasting and celebration. Stella was looking forward to it. She knew she would feel the absence of Camilla more acutely for the presence of the others, but she loved the thought of three generations round one table, her sons together, the strength of kinship, the solidity it meant, if only for a while. She would roast the Easter lamb in the Italian style, as her mother had done and her grandmother before her, and Felix would paint Easter eggs, even if he did so now only to please her.

Felix, that Friday evening, crossed another day off his chart and contemplated time. Six whole days. Two of these days elongated by the collapse of normal structure—on Saturday mornings there were lessons, but Sundays were an interminable wasteland to cross and Wednesday, being the final day of term, would be given over to house competitions. It was a mystery to Felix why there was so much battling for place. House rugger, house swimming, house drama, house singing; what was it supposed to teach? Of late he had become interested in entomology, especially in ants. The cleverness of these scuttling things had impressed him. He had observed their teamwork and the way they tackled the challenge of transporting creatures so much bigger than themselves to the hungry companions back home in their nests. A beetle to an ant? Like a blue whale to a minnow, Felix thought. It would be absolutely no use if the ants held competitions to see which team got to carry off the dinner; they ate because they worked together, like prehistoric hunters killing mammoths. If their hunts had been arranged by prep schools, they would all have starved.

Felix smiled grimly at the picture in his mind of a house mammoth-hunting competition. But it didn't help. There was still this eon to get through. Eon. He said the word out loud. It sounded as it should do, like a howl. A yawning chasm of six days. Adults would think that was no time at all, a mere blink, but it was time enough for God to have made the whole entire world. The light and the darkness, the fish of the sea, the fowl of the air, and every creeping thing that creepeth on the earth. Ants. Except, of course, he didn't. As everybody knows, from the fossil record.

An eon. Infinity. A thought to make you dizzy. Lying on the ground, looking up into the sky, imagining an endless space, an endless time, gave you the same feeling that you got on the flying waltzers at the fair, the same sick lurch and the sense that nothing was quite steady. Lying on the ground, with the whole world spinning round you, you probably looked like an ant in the eyes of God. If God was looking. If God was there. Which Felix suspected he was not.

Being a ten-year-old at this school was like being a creeping thing upon the earth, or one of those small creatures that must have had to spend their whole lives hiding while enormous dinosaurs stamped round, roaring and thundering away, miles above their heads. A leptictidium, perhaps. Felix's life was spent scurrying from lesson to lesson, from meal to meal, from games field to study room, hoping he would not be stopped or noticed.

Alice Armitage was also counting the days, although she did not keep a chart. Three weeks from yesterday, and Fraser would be home. She and Larry still referred to the bedroom Fraser had shared with his brother as the boys' room, even if neither son had slept in it for years. But it still had some of their things in it—football boots, Scalextric, a collection of cassette tapes that no one would ever play again. In the cupboard was a tidy stack of colored plastic boxes full of toys that Mrs. Armitage was keeping for grandchildren. She and Larry hoped there'd be some soon. Stewart had been with his Emma for a long time, having already gone through one sad and short-lived marriage. Perhaps the recollection of that failure was what was stopping him from tying the knot with Emma. If so, that was sad. Mrs. Armitage remembered the wedding vividly, Stewart's new mother-in-law making as much fuss as if it were a royal marriage instead of two young people barely out of their teens and a reception in the village hall. That silly girl had not been local—she had met Stewart at college—and, quite understandably, she'd wanted to be married in her own church rather than the one in which Alice and Larry Armitage had worshiped for thirty-something years. The Armitages did not mind. There's one God, as they often said, and he doesn't care what brand of place you kneel in.

A white veil, yellow roses, baby's breath. And less than two years later that girl had hightailed it and run off with someone she liked better. Or fancied at the time, perhaps. Poor Stewart. He had been very low. But he had cheered up now with Emma.

Fraser's girlfriend Stephanie was lovely. Mrs. Armitage quite understood that he could not have asked her to marry him before he went to Afghanistan, that he did not want to put her under pressure, even though they had been living together for three years, on and off, when he was not in barracks. But maybe, when he got back. Maybe he'd feel that it was time to settle. When he got back. When he got back.

She opened the door of the boys' room and looked in. Take care, love, she said to the bed on the left, with its neatly folded duvet. Silly cow, she said then, to herself. Talking to yourself's the first sign of madness.

At Mr. Kalinowski's earlier that afternoon, Mrs. Armitage had come on quite a scene. The poor, poor duck; he was so upset, and indeed no wonder—wounded dignity hurt more than wounded flesh. He was trying to clean the mess off the carpet when she arrived and would never have opened the door to her, him in his underpants, if she had not persevered. When he had not answered the first ring, she had given him a minute or two before trying again. Then she grew quite worried. If Mr. Kalinowski had been going out that afternoon, Alice Armitage would have known. It would have been a red-letter day for him and he would have told her. As it was, he went out once a month to a Polish ex-servicemen's club in Ruislip to which a fellow veteran would drive him. And he went to church. Otherwise he had very few engagements, and so Mrs. Armitage pushed open the letter box and called through it, then started banging on the door.

Eventually Mr. Kalinowski opened it, a tea towel clutched around his waist. Alice saw he had been crying. The smell in the sitting room informed her of the accident, without the need for words. It happened so quickly, Mr. Kalinowski said. My leg was hurting. I couldn't get out of my chair . . .

Never mind, love, she said. These things happen. It's not the end of the world. Have you got some Flash? I'll have the carpet clean in no time; you just pop along and change.

Mrs. Armitage rinsed the old man's trousers in the sink and put them in his washing machine. Then she had made them both a cup of tea. Mr. Kalinowski was still a little shaky, but composed. She swilled Dettol round the sink. He kept things very nicely, she noticed, glancing round the tiny kitchen.

I'd be lost without you, Mrs. Armitage, he said, as she was leaving.

Now Mrs. Armitage was looking forward to the evening. Old friends who had moved away to Suffolk were coming back to visit, and they all were going out to a restaurant. She loved the luxury of a meal she had not had to cook. It was a good restaurant, newly opened on Battersea Bridge Road—real food, not vacuum-packed and micro-waved; lamb shanks and sea bream, goats' cheese souf-flés, duck confit. Anticipating dinner, a nice bottle or two of wine and the pleasures of friendship reaffirmed, Mrs. Armitage went to her bedroom to get dressed.

Other people were marking days. Kiti Mendoza was organizing a Facebook event for Easter Sunday, when, if you could trust the notice in that stupid church, the cross would be unveiled. People were going to gather in the church and afterward they'd have a picnic in the park. It was a holiday weekend. She was not on duty. A party in the park, those disposable barbecues that were not expensive, a sort of carnival, like there was at home; something to look forward to at last.

Every morning of that week Mary-Margaret went to mass. She took her place in a pew toward the back, went to Com-munion, knelt quietly, left as soon as mass had ended, and did not stop to talk to Father Diamond, as she would have done before. She did not try to enter the Chapel of the Holy Souls. But, as she stood or sat or knelt through the familiar incantations, her whole being was focused on one thing. Although her lips apparently moved in prayer, it was nothing more than reflex, the mouthing of unapprehended words. She went through the motions like a ventriloquist's doll. Inside her head her own voice spoke its real meanings: love and longing, desire, fidelity and passion. She transmit-ted them telepathically to Him.

*

Passion Sunday. Father Diamond looked bleakly at the calendar. Passion Sunday, Palm Sunday, the threshold to Holy Week or the entrance to a tunnel, the mouth of a deep well. This year, more than ever before, Father Diamond doubted his own strength. Did he have the stamina, or indeed the will, to plunge through that door into the week ahead, to suffer each day's events all over again, to walk the weary Stations of the Cross in the footsteps of the Lord? Once, he would have held on to the promise of Easter as a traveler on a winter's night might fix his gaze on a lamp burning in a distant window, the light promised to an exile on return. The glory and the triumph of the Resurrection would have shone out like a fire on which his Lenten sacrifices would be burned, together with the petty deprivations, the insults, the disappointments, the trials of the flesh of forty days. All these would be last year's ashes, consumed by the conquering flame. But this year he could feel no sense of hope. The whole of life seemed as thin and dull as his Lenten diet: black coffee, unbuttered toast, pieces of fish that he unhatched from plastic casings, like mutant embryos entangled in their cauls.

For years Father Diamond had been forswearing animal flesh and the products of flesh in Lent. He took no sweetenings or alcohol either. Usually he appreciated the increased clarity of mind, the sharpened edge, that these small restrictions gave him. They brought him nearer to the desert saints he venerated, who lived their solitary lives in parched, high places; in the salt lands without name; in wilderness, concentrated on prayer alone and close to God. This year he experienced only hunger. Hunger of the acid, nauseous kind and a sort of tiredness; sensations as flat and as discreditable as a habitual drunkard's headache.

Passion Sunday was particularly hard. All those raised hopes dashed and celebratory voices silenced, the sweet hosannas on the lips of children stilled. How could Christ have borne it, riding to Jerusalem in triumph through adulatory crowds who strewed His way with branches and with cloaks, knowing He would die an agonizing death in days?

Father Diamond did not for a single moment equate his suffering with Christ's. He knew that in the scales of pain his own weighed no more than a flake of ash. But he knew he was suffering nonetheless. The problem was that diagnosis gave no clue to cause. Why, suddenly, this year, should his life seem so sad and stagnant when nothing outwardly had changed and his circumstances were the same as they had been for twenty years? Not having an answer, he was afraid. The black hole of the week ahead might be the gaping jaws of hell. How could he force himself to go there, drag one foot after another, plod inexorably onward into darkness? And yet, how could he not? What choice had he? He missed Father O'Connor, who was not due back for another three weeks. In the meantime he must hang on to the liturgical routine as a seafarer in a storm clings to the handrail of the deck; he must mark the days and plead for strength.

Red vestments for Palm Sunday. The color of spilled blood. Blood matted on a crown of thorns, beading on a wounded head.

*

Fidelma woke in the dead of night, her heart thudding hard against its buried cage of bone. Darkness pressed her down, surrounded her, piled up in her mouth and throat. She could not breathe. She could not see. The thunder of her racing heart was the sound of galloping death, or maybe she was dead already. She was gasping, choking, fighting to cough the darkness out, fighting for her breath.

Coming to her senses, she knew it was that dream again. Her nightdress was soaked with sweat, even her sheets were wet. Oh God Almighty what a struggle it was even to sit up in bed, let alone to get clean out. She heaved and squirmed, leaned her bulk on one arm, pressed down with one leg, until at last she sat upright. The light switch was to hand. Not again, she thought, wearily. It came so often now. She knew from dreary experience there was no use haring after sleep; it would have flown toward the dawn.

All through the long hours that followed, Fidelma sat, propped unevenly by pillows, trying to calm her breathing, to steady herself against encroaching fear. But it lapped against her anyway. This room might as well double as her coffin. She would never get out of it again. There would be no touch now that could reconcile her to her flesh. Her mouth was full of fear; it had the taste of earth and ashes.

Azin Qureshi found his mind returning to Stella Morrison even as he went about the ordinary business of a weekend—taking his sons to football on Saturday morning, mending a broken light fitting, catching up on work. It was not that the dinner party had been particularly memorable. His wife's professional life was sociable and Azin was used to accompanying her to a lot of dreary functions. That evening in Battersea had been pretty much what he had expected: middle-aged and middle-class people bewailing the state of the world, or at least its schools and ski slopes, over too many bottles of what they were pleased to call "ordinary" claret. People just like him, as a matter of fact. Theirs was his world too. But Stella had not seemed to fit it as precisely as she should. He couldn't put his finger on the reason why. Outwardly she was no different from other women of her type. She was beautiful, certainly, in a distracted way, but then so was his wife Jenny, more so, with her elegantly cropped blond hair and supermodel figure. By contrast Stella was will-o'-the-wisp and indefinable, all strands and tendrils and impossible to pin down, a figure in a graveyard seen through mist. It irritated Azin that she should haunt him.

One reason why she might, Azin supposed, was the inconclusive conversation they had had about the absurdity of visions. He had observed Stella then, seen how she was about to speak but then held back, seen her almost imperceptible withdrawal from the others, her distance from her husband. His life was full of words; silence was beguiling.

Mary-Margaret in her room, oblivious of her mother, was full of fear too. In the early morning she knelt beside her bed. The day was coming closer; she was eager and impatient but she was also deeply anxious: what would He ask her to do? Would she be strong enough for the task? Lord, I am not worthy to receive you, she prayed over and over again. But only say the word and I shall be healed. Only say, only say the word, only, my own darling, only say one word, but say it straight to me.

Stella Morrison woke to a still morning and the call of birds. With each day and its small new freight of light, their songs grew stronger, as if they were members of an orchestra emerging one by one from hibernation, tuning up with caution, trying out a few notes before releasing the full range of their sounds.

Otherwise it was very quiet. Rufus had left yesterday for New York. Stella stretched diagonally across the bed. Where Rufus would have slept the sheet was smooth and cool; she slid a foot luxuriously along it. There was a whole day and night ahead of her with no one in it and nothing to do but please herself. And tomorrow she would have Felix back.

Stella got out of bed and drew the curtains. Last night the sky had been clear, obsidian-hard, the stars like sharpened points of steel, auguring a frost. But a west wind must have changed the weather's mind; this morning was more gentle, there was the promise of sunshine, ice transubstantiated into mist. A whole day ahead and the countryside around her wakening from winter, pushing out fresh shoots, scented with sap and rain.

Stella had many mornings on her own but fewer uninterrupted days. Having had no supper yesterday, she was hungry now. The kitchen of the cottage was as orderly and still as only a room that has been left by a sole occupant can be. Everything was in its place as it had been the day before; if the small creatures of the night had passed through in the dark hours, they had left no trace behind. There was apple juice in the fridge pressed locally from the fruit of nearby orchards: Worcester Pearmain on the label. The juice was very cold and sweet and cloudy; she swallowed it as thirstily as if the night had been a desert. Apple scent, breaking on her tongue.

A boiled egg in a blue cup, a jar of clear honey. Stella held the jar up to the light; in it the honey glowed like melting amber. She laid the table properly for her breakfast—a pale blue linen napkin, milk in a white jug. From time to time Stella's unobserved habits gave her pause. Perhaps I was never made to be a wife, she thought. Although I would rather not have lived than not have been a mother. These little rituals—the knives and teaspoons carefully placed, the twin triangles of toast—these were the rituals of a woman on her own. If there were a watcher hidden in the corner cupboard, Stella wondered, spying on me through the keyhole, would I be ashamed? Would it be more normal, on my own, to eat my breakfast quickly, standing up, with my attention on the radio or the television news, as Rufus would? Yet the fact is that I *am* unobserved. And small ceremonies afford great comfort. The ordinary miracle of an egg.

Rufus had, as he had promised, set aside almost the whole of Tuesday for her. And Monday evening too. Together time, he said. I owe it to you, don't I? She cooked dinner for them in the cottage; he lit a fire in the sitting room and set a good bottle of wine to warm before it. The next day they went to Kimmeridge and walked the miles of coast from there to Lulworth Cove. He held her hand the whole way and talked of his aspirations and his plans. He'd probably come too late to politics ever to make it as Prime Minister, he supposed. But he'd give it a good shot in the cabinet, after the election. And after that, who knows? Probably he'd get bored of politics, as he had of banking. But having been a government minister was a pretty good springboard. Europe? The World Bank? Ambitious, restless Rufus. Or, he said to Stella with a grin, we could chuck it all in and sail around the world together, thee and me, a second honeymoon.

Afterward they had lunch in a pub chosen by Rufus for its obscurity, so that he would not be recognized. It was obscure for a reason, Stella thought, as the reek of chip fat settled on her hair. But it was also warm and friendly and sustained Rufus's good humor; they had not been out together for some time.

Let's have coffee at home, Rufus had suggested. It's not likely to be drinkable in this place, jolly charming though it is. Stella knew when they got back that he would want to go to bed. Remember how we used to make love in the afternoons? he'd say. Before the kids came. We've just got time before the taxi. Wasn't I clever to make sure that I was booked on the late flight?

Stella remembered. She remembered making love in the mornings and most of the night as well. In the beginning she had thought their lovemaking would be more fulfilling when it was less frantic—when Stella was Rufus's adulterous secret, there had been an element of desperation in their meetings. Much later, when they had put the mis-cry of his divorce behind them and were settling into their own marriage, they made love regularly and often, but for Stella it never became the passionate experience she had hoped it would be. She blamed herself for that. Everything that Rufus did—eating, drinking, talking, walking—he did with great dispatch: why should it be any different in bed? When Stella and Rufus walked anywhere together, she had to quicken her steps almost to a run if she wanted to keep pace with him. Speed and efficiency were intrinsic to her husband. That he brought the same qualities to sex should not have come as a surprise. And now, although he was still businesslike about it and would fit it into his schedule when he could, as he had done the day before, that schedule was too full to leave much room.

Love in the mornings, in the afternoons . . . well, one could live without it. It was not as if there was a choice. Stella had found a compensating pleasure in the intense physicality of the relationship with her children, in the days when they were small. There had been a lover's joy in the touch of them, in the grace and ease with which they had embraced her, the softness of their knees and elbows before they were roughened by hard use.

Felix would still allow her to hug him and to stroke his hair. He would not do so for much longer. Before he went to boarding school, his days began in Stella's bed, where he would slide in beside her in the mornings to ask the questions that came immediately to mind when he woke up, or to speculate about the hours ahead. He did not do that now. And it was quite correct, as Stella knew, that he had made this little distance of his own. It was the same as his new rules about the bathroom. Once, bath time had been a good time for communication with the children. Then, one by one, inevitably, as they grew older, they began to shut and lock the bathroom door. It was strange, in a way, that bodies you once knew as intimately as your own should later be kept hidden from you. Stella had known and loved every tiny portion of her children—the insides of their ears, the gaps between their toes; she had felt each emergent milk tooth with a finger. She had loved her children purely, wholeheartedly, without inhibition, in a way that she could not have extended to an adult's body.

As her children progressed to adulthood, they rightly closed the doors on this unembarrassed closeness. In the changing rooms of the gym where Stella went, women who were strangers to each other thought nothing of being naked. If they looked at one another it was only to reassure themselves through comparison: she is fatter than I, her breasts are saggy. But Camilla would not take off her clothes in front of Stella. Stella would never again see the naked bodies of her sons. Unless they were dead, she thought with sudden horror. Dead and laid out on a marble slab.

Stop this. These sentimental, morbid thoughts. Evolution was a fitting thing, and Stella recognized it. She expected her relationships to change. It was her great fortune that Barnaby, Camilla and Felix stayed close to her in their own ways, were open with their thoughts and feelings. But even so. When they were really grown and gone—to careers and households of their own, to marriages—what then? She would necessarily be peripheral to their lives. Then would she be an aging woman on her own, talking to herself as she was doing now, comforting herself with toast and milk jugs? Or a woman still married to a man she could no longer love?

The uninterrupted day began to seem too long. Do something useful with yourself, Stella admonished sternly. Stop moaning. Think of Mrs. Armitage.

She decided to do some gardening. The small path at the front could do with weeding. After a while she felt more cheerful. The writhing worms and the shy leaves, the thin tendrils of young roots, earth just beginning to be warm, a counterweight to somber thoughts. There were grape hyacinths, and blossom on the damson.

In the late afternoon she went for a walk. A lane at the edge of the village led uphill through woods and, on the other side, to a small lake. When she got there the light was fading, the water silvery and still. The trees on the far shore like a bank of smoke or a mass of gauze, still leafless, only the tallest branches distinct against the sky. Two swans drifted close together in the gathering darkness, pale as moth wings, pale as falling snow.

No one else was there. If there were, would that voice speak? Standing on the lakeshore, with tears in her eyes, Stella called to it. There was no sound, or answer, but on her own, in the silence, after a while, she found a kind of peace.

Say the word, say the word, Mary-Margaret urged. She was on her knees in the Church of the Sacred Heart, waiting for the morning mass. Wednesday. Three days to go. Last night she dreamed He came to her and kissed her softly; she pressed her fingers to her mouth in memory of Him, touched them to where His mouth had been. He had given her a folded sheet of paper. She opened it and there was writing on it, but she could not read the words.

She was making herself ready. Most of the day and half the night she spent in prayer. The only time she stopped was when she was with Shamso. Already they had made a routine for themselves. Every day Mrs. Abdi collected Shamso from his nursery and brought him home for lunch. Then she popped him across the corridor to Mary-Margaret. Even though the school holidays had started, the older Abdis had some kind of day care in the afternoon. Only Shamso and the baby didn't—maybe because they were too young. Mary-Margaret had not understood Mrs. Abdi's explanation but, in any case, she was more than happy to look after Shamso whenever she was asked. She'd gladly have the whole pack of them, in fact—Samatar, Bahdoon, Sagal, Hodan, and Faduma too—but they had other things to do and, truth to tell, it was Shamso she loved most. He seemed to love her too. Now, when his mum dropped him at Mary-Margaret's, he didn't give her so much as a backward glance. Cheerfully as anything he'd scamper up to Mary-Margaret, his little fingers wriggling in the pocket of her fleece, where he knew that she kept sweets for him—chocolate drops or Smarties. As long as he had something in his mouth, Shamso was content.

Yesterday it had been warm enough to go outside to play. Although Shamso couldn't walk very far on his little legs and the new baby seemed to have sole use of the buggy, he could just about get to the park. There were swings there, and a pond, with ducks. Mary-Margaret took some scraps of bread. The poor mite didn't have a clue at first—had he never fed ducks before?—and kept putting the stale crusts in his mouth. So Mary-Margaret broke off some bits and chucked them in the direction of the birds, bringing them at once toward her in a great splash and cluck and clack of wings. And Shamso was thrilled! She had to hold on to him really tightly to stop him throwing himself into the water with the scraps of bread. Gorgeous hair your little boy has, remarked a passing woman, and Mary-Margaret was so proud. She scooped him up and hugged him until he squirmed to be put down; oh he was adorable, so sweet and so delicious.

This afternoon she would have him again. Excitement swelled up in her like water under pressure—she felt her blood flow faster—her whole world was about to change and it was already filled with love. She was willing and her lamp was full, like the wise virgins'. When the bride-groom came He would not find her wanting. Three more days.

On her way home she'd nip into the shops and pick up something special. She hadn't been paying her mum much heed of late. The image of Fidelma wedged into her chair and staring blankly at the window swam to mind. What would her mother like? Mary-Margaret thought of choco-late cake, dark and rich with chocolate-fudge topping. Or those things with layers of custard cream and pastry. White icing on the top. Her mother would love that. You couldn't fit them in your mouth, all that thick cream oozing out and squishing. Shamso would enjoy one too. Mary-Margaret laughed at the thought of Shamso covered in cream, the doll, the precious poppet.

*

Mrs. Armitage was celebrating too. Two weeks today. And for Fraser only one more week, in fact. Then he'd be going to Malta for a debrief, or was it decompression? A week of that, whatever it was, then home. The icing on her cake was that on getting back today, there had been a letter on the doormat. Imagine. She'd crawled in, wearier than usual—it had been a hard day at the depot with two of the regulars off sick and that waste of space who called herself the boss getting her knickers in a twist, and Mrs. Armitage did hope she wasn't coming down with the same bug. She ached as if she'd gone twelve rounds with Big Frank Bruno.

Dragging herself up the garden path she'd also hoped that Larry was in but then remembered he had gone to Croydon. A pity. No one could be nicer to come home to than old Larry. He'd have made a cup of tea and given her a neck rub. He was brilliant at that. He'd never been a man exactly liberal with words or given to romantic gestures; it was as if all his sensitivity and love was gathered in his fingers. Magic hands, Mrs. Armitage would tell him. He knew where the pain was without you even telling.

But just when she was feeling sorry for herself, there was that letter waiting. It wasn't very long, mind. Weather getting filthy hot, *filth's* the word, can't wait for a real shower, tell Dad mine's a pint on April the twenty-second!

It didn't have to be long. Fraser was like his father, economical with words; the point was that he had written. Those ballpoint letters had been formed by her son's hand. Mrs. Armitage kissed the paper they were on, feeling a little silly. Then she left the letter on the table in the hall for Larry, and put the kettle on.

❋

Fidelma and her daughter faced each other over a paper bag of cakes and a bottle of Irish Cream liqueur. For Mary-Margaret, when she shopped, cost was the chief consideration. Ends must be made to meet on income support and a disability allowance, and consequently she was careful. Always bought own-brands and Basics. But once in a while she did leave room for a bottle in her basket. She was drawn to things that reminded her of her heritage, with green fields on the labels and words on them like *cream*. *Cream* was a word that tasted of itself, she thought, and filled the mouth exactly like the real thing.

Mary-Margaret got home just in time for Shamso. Fidelma was asleep, so she hid the cakes away, as a nice surprise. When he arrived, Shamso made quacking noises, to her great delight. Of course then she had to take him to the park. Everything was a new pleasure, when you were with a child. Things you'd seen a million times before—the berries on a dusty bush, a cat on the pavement, a sparrow in a puddle flicking water from its wings—were fresh discoveries to Shamso. Even the lifts in the block excited him. Every time they went in one, Mary-Margaret had to hoist him up and help him push the right button with his finger. It took forever to get to the park because he had to stop and examine everything he saw along the way. He also had a tendency to pick up whatever he found and put it in his mouth, so Mary-Margaret really had to watch him. But she didn't mind. She had all the time in the world for him, or at least for the moment.

When they got back from the ducks, Mary-Margaret gave Shamso his pastry slice but Fidelma, who had just eaten a packet of Jaffa Cakes, wasn't particularly hungry. We'll save them for tea then, shall we? Mary-Margaret said. Both women watched Shamso eating. He picked up the cake with both hands and rammed it in the general direction of his mouth, leaving more around it than inside, as Mary-Margaret observed. Mrs. Abdi looked surprised to find him quite so sticky when she turned up to take him back. It might be an idea to give me some spare clothes for him, Mary-Margaret suggested, but Mrs. Abdi didn't understand. Well, I suppose I could have a look in Oxfam next time I'm there, Mary-Margaret said. It gave her a shiver of pleasure to think of buying clothes for Shamso. Proper little shirts and trousers, not the mismatch of girls' things he seemed to have. And undershirts. Sweet little warm white undershirts. She would clear out a drawer for him in her bedroom and fill it with a pile of neatly folded, washed and ironed clothes. And nappies? She hadn't yet had charge of Shamso long enough to need to change one. But it couldn't be that difficult, could it?

Now Shamso had gone and the women were alone. My hip is bad today, Fidelma said. Have you got any of that jelly stuff? Mary-Margaret asked. You said it helps?

Yes. I'll rub some of it on later. Can't be bothered now. Sausages?

And chips? And there's the cakes. Also, look, wait. She went to the kitchen for the bottle of Irish Cream and gave it with a flourish to her mother.

What did you buy that for? Fidelma asked. We still have the whiskey.

It was on offer, Mary-Margaret said. She disliked the harsh taste of the whiskey, the way it made the skin feel rough all the way down your throat. This other kind of drink was softer. Have some, Ma.

I will, when I have the chips on. Fidelma used her walker to hoist herself out of her chair. Her legs were crampy. She had no need for shoes, only for slippers; even so her feet felt squashed. She sighed.

It was their agreement that Fidelma cooked and Mary-Margaret did the shopping. She was surprisingly good at it, Fidelma often thought, for a lass who could scarcely count, let alone add up. Well, maybe that was not quite fair. Of course Mary-Margaret could count, and read and write as well; it was just that she was slow, as she had always been; a struggler, she was, at school. Fidelma as a child had been much sharper. She sometimes wondered what she might have done, if she could have stayed at school. Maybe she would have been a writer. She always did like stories, words.

Fidelma shuffled to the kitchen. It had a window that faced the same way as the main room's; lights were coming on quickly in the windows of the tower block opposite, one by one, it seemed, a ripple of lights, wimpling like sun on moving water. She put the oil on to heat. The bangers looked too much like bits of her own self for comfort. Clammy, bulging, mottled. She pushed the notion away. They'd be fine when they were done. She sipped the drink that Mary-Margaret poured her.

The women ate sitting at right angles to each other. Having dished the food onto plates, Fidelma left it in the kitchen and went back to her chair; it was easier to manage if she didn't have her hands full. Mary-Margaret brought her her plate when she had settled down, then she fetched her own.

They had the television on but this evening Mary-Margaret was chatty. She poured more of the Irish Cream into her glass. Later I'll make tea, she said, but this is lovely; it'll go down very nicely with the vanilla pastry slices.

It's pretty, isn't it, Ireland? Look at these fields, with the cows in them.

Fidelma laughed. There were no green fields around her when she was a girl. Only the stony hillside and the wild moorland; the sand and the endless sea. But there had been flowers, she remembered, on the hillside. Orchids, meadow-sweet and harebells; the white harebells were rarer; finding one was supposed to bring you luck. Well, even if she had stumbled on a field of them, they would not have made a difference, she supposed. After the hillside, the dark streets of the town. Straight lines of sad gray houses, like a row of tombstones, hunched against the rain. And the home the sisters kept the saddest of them all. The biggest too, tower-ing over all the others, blocking out what light there was in the narrow street.

Any day now Father O'Connor will be back, Mary-Margaret said, out of the blue. He said that he'd be back soon after Easter.

Fidelma said she had no concern with the whereabouts of the priest. After she spoke she wondered if that was true. He had been away a good six months now; it was just pos-sible she missed him. Although she never asked him to, he turned up once a month or so; we've got to stick together, he would say, us exiles.

An exile. Well so she was, in every way.

Mary-Margaret went on watching *Emmerdale*. After a while she said, it's a bit weird, how we call them Father. I never thought of that before. I mean, you'd call Father Diamond Father even though you're older than him. Still, it would be even funnier if you called him Son! She laughed at her joke.

If he was the Pope, you'd have to call him Daddy, Fidelma said. Papa. That's what the word means.

Mary-Margaret looked confused. I thought I would have to call him Holiness, she said. Your Holiness. Not Papa!

She tasted the word again. Papa. I wonder where Shamso's papa is, she said. Or if he has one. But he must. I mean she is Mrs. Abdi. There has to be a Mr. Abdi too.

Well, I do hope so, Fidelma said. And her with all those kids.

Does it make a difference, having lots? So if you have loads of children you have to have a husband but if you have just one . . . ? she stopped. She topped up her glass and Fidelma's and went to take the empty plates into the kitchen.

Fidelma sighed again. Mary-Margaret had been an incurious little girl, accepting all that she was told as gospel. I got you all by myself, Fidelma used to tell her and, later, when Mary-Margaret was too old for fairy tales of storks and changelings, she said her dad was dead. As, indeed, he might be, Fidelma told herself in mitigation of the lie; for all she knew, he might be dead.

Mary-Margaret came back with clean plates for the vanilla slices. They ate them in silence. Waves of sweetness on the tongue, thick white icing, yellow cream, the pastry yielding to the softness of its filling.

I used to think you were a blessed virgin, Mary-Margaret said suddenly. When I was a tiny child. She licked her fingers to pick up a flake of icing from her plate.

Fidelma started. Virgin? she said.

That would have made me a bit like Jesus, Mary-Margaret went on. Born without an earthly father. "How shall this be, seeing I know not a man?" You know. But that was before I understood about you being a widow. The poor widow and her mite.

I think the mite in that case was a coin, Fidelma said. Sweet Jesus, here she was, this great big lump of a girl, not all that far off now from being a middle-aged woman. Simple, she might be, but not that simple, surely? Couldn't she put two and two together? She watched enough TV, for goodness sake. Fornication, adultery and incest, everywhere you looked. It was time, Fidelma thought, that Mary-Margaret faced facts.

I was never married, she said. So I am not a widow. You have to have been a wife first, and I was never that.

Mary-Margaret looked at her for a while. Then she smiled kindly. It doesn't matter now, she said. It's only a shame he died so young, before you could be married.

She was quiet after that, her attention seemingly held by the television. What about that tea you promised? Fidelma asked her when the program finished. I'm tired, Mary-Margaret said. I'll make you a cup if you want one but I am off to bed.

When she had gone, Fidelma turned the television off and sat in darkness. Not for the first time she mourned the absence of a fire. If there were a fire, she would have something to stare at other than the window. She thought of the hearth at home, the scent of it, kept burning night and day although smoored at night with ashes. Every morning her mother would scoop a shovelful of glowing embers from that fire to carry to the range in the next room, a dangerous load, the glint of it, the heat, the gold-vermilion. In this way the fire in the range was resurrected, the other sparking it to life with its dying embers in an everlasting rhythm, as if the two were kin, the open fire the parent of the fire that was pent up in its cast-iron casing. Fire spirits. Guardians of the house.

She missed them. For its brief warmth she struck a match and lit a cigarette. There was a place in her chest which the smoke rasped. This room, her casing, was a square box merely, lacking internal focus. There were a hundred and ten exactly like it in this tower—five on every story of the twenty-two. Think what chimneys they would have had to build, if they had put a fireplace in every flat—chutes deeper than the deepest wells, vertical black tunnels in which a lost child would be trapped forever.

The inside of her mouth felt as if it had been brushed with fat. She could taste the yellow filling of the cake. It had been kind of Mary-Margaret to buy them. They had never had all that much to say to one another—sometimes Fidelma thought they were less like mother and daughter than like prisoners serving out life sentences in a double cell—but of late the girl had seemed more than usually caught up in her own world.

Even convicts forced to live as partners in a box six foot by ten must have their secrets. Even if, on the surface, everything was known—each fart, each breath, each mouthful—still no one could make them share the spaces in their heads.

Fidelma knew Mary-Margaret's routines, her likes, her dislikes, but she had small insight into her mind. And Mary-Margaret had still less understanding of Fidelma's. But no one does, Fidelma thought. No one ever has. Since the early days of childhood, her life had been lived in secrecy and silence, in the private places of her soul, where there was safety, freedom, the infinity of the open sky, the glistening strand, the raging sea. And just as well, these days, when there was nowhere else that she could go, for this fireless room was really nothing other than the grave.

Secrecy and silence. She thought back to the getting of Mary-Margaret, the twilit times, coupling quickly in his curragh, beached, always with an ear to footsteps on the sand. The smell of salt and fish on him, the taste of salt, and scales like sequins, lodged like fairy coinage underneath his nails. Sticking to her afterward, as if by loving him she might turn into a mackerel or a mermaid, pink flesh quickening to pearl and gray and silver, gleaming in the ripples of the dark.

Oh God, oh God, oh God, Almighty God, the sheer beauty of the thing. How his eyes closed and he gasped, how she hungered and she tightened for him in her secret place, like a creature of the rock pools, an anemone, clinging onto her desire. It was hunger, no other word for it, hunger that you did not know that you could feel until you'd felt it—and then, well then, it never left you. Ah the way a woman aches inside and wants him deeper and, oh God, the helpless shiver when she has him and the shattering delight, spreading out in circles, halos, as if the core of her were liquid and he the stone thrown in it.

Oh God. He was so beautiful, that boy. Beautiful. And already married. By the age of eighteen he was a married

man, by the age of nineteen the father of a . . . Ah stop. What
was he to do about it? He had simply been there when she
went back to the old place for the last time that last summer, a boy she'd known, friends with her big brother, they
had all walked to school together over the flaggy places, all
the children of the strand. Their bare feet in the summer
sinking into warm bog water, meadowsweet and clover. He
was there when she came back but only as the stunted trees
were there, and the sheepfolds or the heaps of stone. A part
of the surroundings, not to be remarked on, that boy who
had always been there, until one night he looked at her and
suddenly she'd seen him and his eyes as gray as winter sea.

There'd been others since, Lord knows, and not for love
but money, most of those. Can there be a more unpleas-
ing smell than dirty money? Their fingers stank of grubby
tenners and fistfuls of dull copper; the same reek on their
trousers, their flies all stained and greasy. Tongues thick
with smoke and lies. She'd do what she had to, except she
would not kiss them. Suck it, bitch. The stink of public toilets, stale clothes, like the stink of jumble sales, and she'd
known those too, God knows.

Fidelma closed her eyes. All those long and weary years.
And the times of freshness so far away and few. His scent
of cold salt water. Peat smoke in his hair and on his clothes,
not the city smoke of pubs and coal and desperation. Her
face against his shoulder, the thick wool he was wearing,
she breathed in peat smoke and salt water. The taste of his
mouth as clean as grass, so sweet his kissing, and his mouth
on hers and signals sent through every vein and every
nerve. Both bodies craving, meeting, crying, shaking like
two birds tumbled in a storm after the great joy they had

shared. The way he gasped, a breath indrawn, a sob almost, the way he closed his eyes.

What happened to him in the end? She would never know. The summer she was there by the seashore with him was the last summer, and the first since she'd been sent away, with Bridget, Maeve and Mary, to the city. Their mother had struggled on awhile, with the younger children: Deirdre, Siobhan and baby Ronan. For the first few years she made the journey to the city every six months or so to see her elder daughters; later she could not afford it. By then Siobhan had joined the others and Deirdre gone to an aunt in Sligo; that last summer there was only Ronan left. Seven years old, he was, that summer. And, all of a sudden, without a word of warning, Mammy took up with a fellow visiting from Toronto, and went back with him when his visit ended, taking Ronan. Promises there were, of course, of airfares and of money, but they never came. And besides, by that time, Fidelma was a mother herself, or about to be.

She must have asked herself a thousand times if she had made the right choice then. And a thousand times supplied the answer. That there was no choice. The boy with the wintry eyes was spoken for already. The Sisters of Unmercy, in their winged veils like crows, would have swooped on the newborn baby as if she were fresh carrion if Fidelma had not shooed them all away. Why had she not handed them the child? God knows. Because the child had not chosen to be born, perhaps? Because of the pleasure in her making? Because there had been love as well as winter in the boy's gray eyes. Because the mite was small and so defenseless and there had been no one else in like need of Fidelma.

And afterward, what then? A ferry into furtive exile. Jumble sales and council offices and tricks in the backs of cars for cash. And the fisher-boy, perhaps the father of a brood, thinking from time to time of his lost daughter. When he was out there, on his own, on the lonely sea. Cold rain on his skin and his small boat pitching; like all fishermen he had never learned to swim.

But would he think; would he remember? Would he taste Fidelma's kisses in the rain? She had been beautiful herself then; lithe and slender as the fish he hunted, skin as white as buttermilk and soft as flower petals. And look what she was now. A mountain of loose flesh, a huge great wobbling heap of blubber, something seen on a butcher's slab in nightmares, quivering and overflowing, fold on fold and layer on layer; the girl she once was now encased in fat, imprisoned and so deeply changed that she might never have been. Flesh that smelled of mold and grease, not meadowsweet and grass. Breasts like the swollen udders of abandoned cows, spread-nippled, thick-veined, bulging.

Yet this monstrous blooming did not mean that hunger had been sated. No, not at all. Hidden in the caverns of the hulk there was that place still yearning, and the terror, and the knowledge that it would never now be filled. No mouth would ever kiss Fidelma's, no man encircled by her eager body cry with pleasure when he came. The only loving she would know again was lovemaking in dreams. And she did feel love in dreams. So intense the feelings, and so real, that the climax washed her up onto the stony shores of wakefulness and left her weeping for lost pleasure and for helplessness, for sadness that it had only been a dream.

*

On Wednesday evening Kiti Mendoza's Auntie Rita had already started cooking for the picnic. She was planning leche flan and coconut cake, adobo, dumplings to be eaten cold, skewers of fried chicken. Would it be possible to roast a suckling pig on one of those baby barbecues? Lumpia were good party food, but could they be reheated? She was looking forward to the day. Whatever about that crucifix— and the truth was she couldn't care less about it one way or another—it was a good reason for a party. And Rita could do with one. A thankless and a tiring life she had, cleaning rooms in a hotel, hoarding the pennies she made to send back home. This distraction was very welcome, this excuse to gather friends together from their scattered community, to cook properly for a change, to share real food. Today she had tasted the promise of summer in the air, the long winter was over at last and she was pleased.

Felix Morrison spiraled in and out of sleep like a sycamore seed caught in a gust of wind. He hovered between sleep and wakefulness as he hovered on the threshold between holiday and term time. He had been counting the days and they had gone so slowly. Tomorrow he would be home. But only twenty-one days later, he would be back at school. In a moment of clarity, in the dead hours of that Wednesday night, Felix saw the years stretching ahead of him like an endless seesaw on which he would never find his balance. He would spend his whole life tossed between looking forward in excitement and looking forward in plain dread.

Was he quite alone, a minute ant in a giant universe, with this sicky feeling? Or did all the other boys now snuffling and sighing in their beds beside him share it too? How would he ever know? Unimaginable it was to strut up to, for instance, Pommeridge, who was the dormitory head, and say: now tell me, Pommeridge, do you live in the present? Or are you always straining for the future?

Could he ask his mother? Tell me how to live today? Just possibly, yes, he could but there might be a danger then that she would ask him why he was afraid. And that would not be good. He did not want to make her sad with that. Ever since he was a little boy, Felix had tried to shield his mother from upset. Which was why he never told her how he cried at night in school. Although, actually, he was quite sure she felt the same for him. Quite probably she cried at night as well, but she would never say so. They were brave for one another, that's just how it was; the way the world worked, maybe, or maybe it was something else.

Maundy Thursday. Father Diamond woke with a sick feeling, as if some sour thing were squatting in his guts. He knew immediately what day it was. Maundy Thursday. The syllables tolled like a death knell. Holy Thursday was the correct new term, but Father Diamond still thought of the day as Maundy. Because he was on his own he was excused some of the customary duties of a parish priest. But there was still so much to do. What for? For an empty church with the altars stripped, for darkness and for nothing.

*

Mrs. Armitage got out of bed with a glad heart. These mornings of bright daylight were still surprise enough to be a wonderful new present, the possession of which gave pleasure every time you thought about it. Opening the window, she sensed the air had changed. After a long winter, spring could be a ditherer, putting one foot forward and then withdrawing it, like a shy child unsure whether to join in with the game. Even when fine, the days of March and early April could hold a taint of winter but today the light was clear. In her tidy garden, forsythia in full bloom was sunshine captured and distilled and the birds were singing as if their little lungs would burst. Honestly, she thought, this is more than just a change of season; it is the whole world breathing a great sigh of relief. Winter has at last let go, Lent is almost over, it will soon be Easter Sunday, Fraser is coming home.

The most delicious smell in the world—fresh toast—was wafting in through the bedroom window from the kitchen below. Larry was up already, making breakfast. Thursday, Friday, Saturday, Sunday, Monday: five whole days unbroken by work, holidays, holy days, with Larry. On Easter Sunday Stewart and his girlfriend would come over; Mrs. Armitage would buy the lamb today. A leg was the traditional thing but she always said you got more value from a shoulder. Better texture, better taste. She had the eggs already. Larry would have bought one for her and hidden it behind his shirts in his side of the cupboard. They always gave up sweets and chocolate for Lent, and things with added sugar, and although neither she nor Larry really had that much of a sweet tooth to be honest, it was nice to look forward to the Easter eggs. She would keep one by for Fraser.

She had a lot to do today. The shopping for the holiday weekend, as she absolutely didn't hold with doing it on Good Friday, even though, apparently, the shops would all be open. She'd pop in to see Mr. Kalinowski and poor Phelim; Antoinette, if she had time. She must make sure that Father D had not forgotten Joan, who would want Communion. And she needed to be sure the house was sparkling clean. It's an animal instinct, she said to herself, to sweep out the burrow in spring. Larry, bless him, would do the windows, if she asked him. This new gift of daylight didn't half show up flyspecks, smears and fingerprints on glass! An image of the soul in the sight of heaven? You're quite the poet in your old age, she told herself and laughed. But first she had the church to do. Although she cleaned it every Thursday, this Thursday was special. Come to think of it, with a small detour, she could go there via the baker's. Pick up some hot cross buns for Father Diamond to eat tomorrow. Father Diamond was shrinking before her eyes, becoming paler and thinner by the week, and he hadn't enough to lose in the beginning. That sharp-faced housekeeper of his evidently didn't feed him. Probably she didn't make the effort when he was on his own; she favored Father O'Connor.

Azin Qureshi woke to the first squawk of his alarm clock and hit the off switch hard before the noise irrevocably disturbed his wife. She had the day off but he was working as usual and was then on call for the whole weekend. Not that it mattered—his family had no particular plans in any case and would probably do what they always did at weekends: watch television, go shopping, go to football practice. His sons would have their friends round and the house would fill with the sound of small boys playing on Nintendos. Jenny claimed her Saturdays as time all to herself; after a hectic working week she certainly deserved a few hours off, a pedicure, her dance class, coffee with a girlfriend. She'd asked people round to supper, Azin now remembered, but as she had recently discovered a service that delivered food to your house all ready to heat up, she wouldn't have to worry about cooking. The food was good but not so slick that you couldn't pretend it was homemade.

When he was a child, bank-holiday weekends had seemed very long and very quiet. Azin could recall a time when shops were shut for days on end, as well as every Sunday. Now, he thought, it was left to a few fanatics in the Scottish Highlands to protest that Sundays should be special. Sabbatarians? Or were those Orthodox Jews? Muslims made it easier—or harder—for themselves by making every day a day of prayer. Fridays, though, had particular significance, now he came to think about it. Good Friday. Azin had forgotten how it got its name. He made a mental note to look it up; it was the sort of thing he should be able to tell his sons.

Meanwhile there was today to deal with. A meeting with the Mental Health Trust, the review of an American psychiatrist's book on depressive illness that he had promised to the *TLS* last week, his notes for a talk at a conference in May, his clinic at the hospital in the afternoon. Patient after patient, the sad, the lonely and the old, those bare forked beings bent beneath the weight of disappointment, disillusion, hopelessness and loss. Azin closed his eyes for a moment and saw them in procession, today's and yesterday's and those who were still to come, straggling in a long line through the years, like pilgrims winding round steep mountain paths, except that they had no common goal. What was it that they would count as cure? Relief from the pain of being human and alone—and no psychiatrist in the world could offer that.

Azin got out of bed. Jenny, with her back to him, on the other side, was lying so still that he knew she was awake and waiting until he left the room. Then she'd burrow deeper into the tangle of bedclothes and keep the day at bay a little longer. She was not one for conversation first thing in the morning. Azin glanced at her bright blond head a little wistfully. It would be nice if she turned over, opened her eyes, and smiled, and stretched her arms up to him; if she would draw him into her warm softness, welcome him inside her without need for words. But she did not move, and he put on his dressing gown and went downstairs to make breakfast for the boys.

Mary-Margaret told her mother at breakfast that she had champagne in her veins instead of blood. Fidelma laughed. They were eating eggy-bread and bacon. Have you ever had champagne? she asked. Mary-Margaret had not, but she knew that it was fizzy. She was simply trying to give her mother a sense of her excitement; she should have saved her breath. But Fidelma's scorn only temporarily tamped down the rising joy. She felt it surge and bubble, her heart was beating fast, her head was light and full of air. Shall I get Father Diamond to bring the Sacrament to you? she asked her mother. Get away, Fidelma said.

After breakfast Mary-Margaret collected her kit together: duster, an awl for scraping out the candle wax, a J-cloth, Pledge. I'm going to do the church, she told Fidelma. Then I'll do the shopping. Is there anything you want me to get? Not that it's the end of the world if I forget stuff. The corner shop is open all the time. Mentally she made a note to stock up for Fidelma. She didn't expect to be around much after this weekend. There'd be interviews and television, apart from anything else. But she'd have to take care of her mother, come what may. She is my cross, she thought. Fidelma reminded her that they had run out of margarine.

On her way down Falcon Road to church Mary-Margaret made plans. The right dress, for a start. How was she meant to be the bride of Christ in Oxfam jeans? She'd have a look on her way back, after the church, before it was time for Shamso.

Felix Morrison, in the front seat of his mother's car on his way home to London, was lapped in warmth and safety. His trunk was in the boot and the old ice-cream container he had scrounged from the school kitchen for his minibeasts was securely wedged in with it. There's a boy in my year who lives in Scotland, he said to his mother. And he has another name for wood lice. Slaters. Don't you think that's funny? Two names for the exact same thing in the same language? I mean it's not like he's speaking Scottish!

There are alternative words for lots of things, Stella said, distractedly. She did not much like to talk when she was driving. Local words, or old ones, especially for animals and plants. Think of *brock* and *badger. Emmet* and *ant. Stinking iris* or *roast-beef plant.*

Stinking iris! I've never heard of those. That would be a cool name for a band. I suppose, two words for one thing, that's all right for flowers and stuff because you can actually see them, you can show the other person what you are talking about even if you don't know the word. Like you could if they were German. But when there are two words for a thing that can't be seen, that's a bit confusing, don't you think?

It can be, Stella agreed. But mostly those words which seem to be almost the same have different shades of meaning. Like *adore* and *love.*

Felix glanced at his mother's profile. Adore and love. Trust and faith. I've never heard anyone call an ant an emmet, he said. Or a badger, brock. They only say that sort of thing in books.

Thursday evening, almost six o'clock. For the past hour Father Diamond had been hearing confessions. Before that he had prepared the church for a solemn mass and made ready the place of reposition in the Blessed Sacrament Chapel. He had already mustered as many male parishioners as he could for the foot washing.

The faithful were arriving. After the purples and tallows of Lent, the whiteness of the vestments, the altar hangings and the candles pierced the eyes with the sharpness of light at the end of a long journey through a tunnel. Father Diamond had covered the crucifix on the altar with a white cloth but left the other crosses and the statues in their purple. Behind the altar the tabernacle was empty, open and unveiled, shocking as an accident, the space revealed within it a space that should never be seen.

> Glory be to Jesus,
> Who in bitter pains
> Poured for me the lifeblood
> From his sacred veins!

the congregation sang. We are gathered here to share in the supper, Father Diamond said in the opening prayer. He put his hands flat on the altar for a moment, to steady himself, to derive some strength from the stone beneath the linen cloth. Comforter, where is thy comforting? Miss Daly stepped up to the lectern for the readings. In her voice was the confidence earned from years of addressing schoolgirls in assembly and understanding the word of the Lord. "It must be an animal without blemish," she read, "a male one-year-old. . . . That night I will go through the land of Egypt and strike down all the firstborn in the land of Egypt, man and beast alike, and I shall deal out punishment to all the gods of Egypt. I am the Lord."

From the pulpit Father Diamond looked down across the upturned faces. He searched for Stella but did not see her. No surprise. He closed his eyes a moment. Self-sacrifice, he said. Self-giving. He does not ask for holocaust and victim but an open ear, an open heart. Love one another as I have loved you. And yes, it's hard.

Seamus and Major Wetherby had both turned out, praise be. There was also Xavier, an occasional Sunday server. Major Wetherby took charge. After the sermon he gestured to the men sitting in the front pew to come forward. Larry Armitage, Mr. Kalinowski, the pale youth who had intimations of a vocation, Danny and Kafui, other regulars. They could not make the twelve. Shuffling a little, looking sheepish, they filed into the sanctuary and sat down on the chairs placed for them. At Major Wetherby's signal, they stooped to take off their right shoes and socks. Mr. Kalinowski, bending, found suddenly he could not reach. Larry, seeing this, took his shoe off for him.

Major Wetherby held a ewer, Seamus a basin, Xavier a stack of towels. Father Diamond knelt down before Kafui, the first man in the row: Kafui raised his foot. Major Wetherby passed the ewer to Father Diamond, who poured water over the foot into the basin, held by Seamus on his left. Xavier passed him a towel. Carefully Father Diamond dried Kafui's foot. He stood up and bowed to the next man, and knelt again, eight feet in a line. The pale boy's toes were long and bony, Danny's as hairy as a goat's, Mr. Kalinowski's twisted and his toenails gnarled.

After Communion Father Diamond, escorted by Seamus and Major Wetherby bearing candles, transferred the Holy Eucharist to the tabernacle in the place of reposition, while the faithful sang:

Word made Flesh, by word he maketh
Very bread his Flesh to be;
Man in wine Christ's Blood partaketh;
And if senses fail to see,
Faith alone the true heart waketh
To behold the mystery.

And, when the mass was ended and he had disrobed, Father Diamond stripped the altar. He extinguished all the candles and the lamps. He emptied the Holy Water stoups. The only light left in the church came from the candles in the place of reposition. A few of the faithful stayed there to watch awhile, and pray. But long before midnight, one by one, they drifted quietly away. Father Diamond snuffed the candles out. Among the shrouded figures, before the naked altars, in the silence, Father Diamond kept vigil by on his own. Facedown on the floor he lay the whole night long, in the darkness of the empty church.

Good Friday. Confessions in the morning in the church. Mary-Margaret O'Reilly was among the early penitents. Bless me, Father, for I have sinned, she whispered through the grille. I have had unkind thoughts about my mother. I have been proud. I have failed to keep my Lenten resolution.

What was your Lenten resolution? Father Diamond asked. To take my tea without milk and sugar, Mary-Margaret said. And so I did, most of the time. But lately . . . tea without is shocking bitter.

Say one Hail Mary, Father Diamond said. And pray for me.

Pray for me, that this bitter cup should pass. He was caught in the inexorable progress of the days. Good Friday. After the penitents had left, the church would empty again and stay silent till the ninth hour, when there was darkness over the whole land. Then the church would fill. The Litany of the Word. The Veneration of the Cross. Holy Communion. Yesterday, today, tomorrow. To the last syllable, the last leaden syllable, of recorded time.

How to bear the reiterated story? The thorns, the whips, the wounds, the broken reed, the broken man stumbling over cobblestones under the weight of his own crossbar, vinegar and hyssop, blood and water spilling from his side. *Eloi, Eloi, lama sabachthani,* why have you forsaken me, O Lord?

The faithful would listen, kneel, sing mournful songs and process one by one to kiss the feet of the corpus on the cross, which Major Wetherby and Seamus would prop against a stool, and guard, taking turns to wipe the lip marks off. I opened the sea before you, but you opened my side with a spear. I am forgotten as a dead man, out of mind, I am like a broken vessel, my bones are wasted away.

I go mourning all the day long.

For my loins are filled with burning;

And there is no soundness in my flesh.

On Friday night Father Diamond slept the sleep of the dead and woke early the next morning, more refreshed. Felix Morrison woke early too and went in search of food for his pet wood lice. Yesterday he had researched their needs. It had been good to learn that they did not require a lid on their container because they could not crawl up the plastic sides. He liked to think that although they were actually captive they would feel free in their well-provisioned world, with the open sky above them. He had also discovered they had lots of other names, apart from slater. And deeply satisfactory they were, these names:

bibble bugs, monkey peas, penny bugs, roly-polys, tiggy hogs. Cud worms and coffin cutters.

Stella woke later to the gentleness of a house shared only with a child. She could hear Felix pottering about downstairs, talking to his wood lice, humming. This enchanting, eccentric child, with his quick imagination and his empathy—it was so good to have him home. And, later today, his brother. Rufus was staying in New York for a party but would be back first thing tomorrow, in time for the feast-day celebration. Meanwhile, there was this peaceful day, and Felix, and nothing much to do but bake a cake and pick up Father Diamond's flowers.

When Felix was a tiny baby, less than a month old, the family had spent a few days in Cornwall, in a hotel by the sea. There had been some confusion with the booking so that the interconnecting rooms they had requested were already taken. To Rufus's annoyance, they had ended up with two rooms on separate floors. Having ruled against leaving the older children on their own, Rufus went in crossly with them. Stella, pretending disappointment that she could not sleep with Rufus, was secretly pleased. Her room faced the sea. She left the curtains undrawn and the windows open; all night the wind blew in, lifting the hair off her face where she lay on the pillow, making billowing white sails of the curtains, blessing the swaddled baby in his cot beside her. The nights were a journey across water and the little room a vessel; sleeping the half sleep of the mother of a newborn child Stella drowsed and woke and dreamed to the rhythm of the sea and the kiss of the wind, feeling there was no one but the two of them in the entire world. Almost it was as if she had been returned with Felix to an airy womb, to complete safety, self-containment, absolute fulfillment. The baby woke and suckled himself back to peaceful sleep; in the morning he was next to her, as warm as a new egg, perfect as apple blossom.

A cake, and flowers. A pistachio cake, she thought, with orange flower icing; green for Easter, green for new life, now the green blade riseth from the buried grain. Fields of our hearts that dead and bare have been. Felix would help her bake it, and they could paint hard-boiled eggs together. She had promised Father Diamond she would arrange the flowers for the church this afternoon: white roses, yellow mimosa, white broom, lilies.

Alice Armitage slept badly. As a woman who did not think of herself as over-imaginative, it disturbed her that her dreams were out of her control. Last night she dreamed that she'd come home from the Good Friday service to find a man in uniform standing on her doorstep. From a distance she thought that it was Fraser. But, coming closer, she'd seen the shoulder flashes and the cap badge; she'd known the uniform was not her son's, and at once she knew what the man had come to tell her. The shock of grief was so intense that it woke her clean out of sleep and left her unsure for a while if she'd been dreaming or awake. The pain left real traces, as if its origin were physical and factual; it was like a promise, or a foretaste, of what Alice would endure if Fraser were to die in Afghanistan. Her firstborn son. Her love and her delight.

A dream is not a premonition, Mrs. Armitage assured herself. It is a dream, and nothing else. Only the ignorant hold with omens. It's natural for a mother to be anxious. But still, but still. Men did die in battlefields on the eve of their return, as they died on their first day of deployment. A twist of fate or, as Fraser would say, sod's law. But not God's law, Alice prayed. Holy Mary, mother of God, who had to watch your own son die, watch over mine and bring him back unharmed in soul or body.

There were different accounts, as Mrs. Armitage was aware, of exactly who was standing at the foot of the cross while the man Jesus died His agonizing, drawn-out death. A plethora of Marys, and mothers of sons, Johns and James, it seems. Mary, blessed among women. There could not be a grief more unendurable than to watch your own child suffer. How could Mary not have hated God when she saw the broken carcass of her son being hauled down from a stick like the tatters of a superseded flag? Who so loved the world that He sent His own son to die upon a cross?

And where was Joseph, while Mary bore the hours of pain? Or the other fathers, come to that? In the end, then as always, women had to take the burden, pick up the broken pieces, wipe away the tears and blood. In sorrow they shall bring forth children and in utter loneliness they shall lay those children in their graves. This night I shall go through the land of Egypt and strike down all the firstborn in the land. But let me not bury my child, please God, not mine, not Fraser, my firstborn son.

Mrs. Armitage sat up and switched on the bedside lamp. Larry was asleep beside her, lying on his back, his mouth a little open, a glaze of dribble in its corner. He stirred in the sudden light and muttered something. Alice? It's nothing, love, she said, and turned the light back off. Lying down again, she wriggled across the bed. Still asleep, he stretched out an arm and drew her closer in. Eventually she slept also, and when she woke in the morning it was with a faint ache only, a memory of pain, as if a migraine suffered in the night had ebbed or an old wound surfaced briefly before burying itself beneath her skin again.

Mary-Margaret was woken by the thudding of her heart. Today, today, today it beat, like a panicked dream, fast as fury, urgent as alarm. She leapt up at once; no time to waste, no slugabed hours, no daydreaming in the warmth and tangle of her sheets this morning. All hands on deck, Mrs. Armitage had said on Thursday, when she was telling everybody what they had to do for Easter. All hands. Mary-Margaret took that to mean she would be expected. Which was to the good, given how peculiar Father Diamond had been since the accident, and Mrs. A so nasty and suspicious. Even though on Thursday Mary-Margaret and Mrs. Armitage had polished, swept and dusted as if their lives depended on the cleanness of the church, it would still need another go this morning. All those people toing and froing—Thursday evening, Friday afternoon—would have left their trails of rubbish. There would be fingerprints on the brass. On this day, of all days, for this holy Vigil, all must be perfect and every inch must shine.

And more than this, much more than this, the statues and the pictures. The moment Mary-Margaret had been waiting for since she fell off the altar had come at last.

Alleluia, at long last. The perfect dress she had found yesterday was hanging from a hook behind the door. Oh God, the waiting had been hard. But now the truth would be revealed and the faithful bathed in radiant light. At last. All hands on deck, Mary-Margaret said out loud. To make ready the way of the Lord. For this is the day the Lord has made. My day. And the Lord's.

She really ought to eat some breakfast. Breakfast like a king and dine like a pauper, wasn't that the saying? Breakfast for the King of Heaven. But she really didn't think that she could take a single mouthful. Her stomach was churning like the white water that frothed and foamed behind a ferry. There was a strange feeling in her head. And her heart still thumping, thumping like a fish caught in a net, like a trapped bird beating on a window, like a mad thing hammering for escape.

Do you think we'll have any more trouble with the 'pilgrims'? Larry Armitage was asking Father Diamond.

Oh, I do hope not, Father Diamond replied. It's been fairly quiet this Passiontide, so far. We've had our regulars and the visitors we would expect; I think the sensation seekers have given up on us . . .

I'm sure that's right, Mrs. Armitage interrupted. These things are nine-day wonders really; the sorts of people who believe that nonsense soon move on to the next sensation and forget the last. She gave Mary-Margaret a look.

But perhaps we ought to keep the door locked, just in case, this afternoon? Stella Morrison will do the flowers at five. Or thereabouts. I think that's what she said. So I'll be around then and will get things organized in time for six o'clock. Then there'll be tomorrow's solemn mass, of course.

Will Mrs. Morrison need a hand? asked Mrs. Armitage.

It's sweet of you to think of it. But I imagine she'll cope. I mean, if she needs someone to deal with her Oasis, I'm her man! I may not be Constance Spry, but I can tell a cabbage from a rose. As long as they're not cabbage roses, I suppose. You're too good really, Mrs. Armitage. We've already trespassed enough on your precious time. And on yours, of course, he added, to Mary-Margaret.

Mrs. Armitage managed a smile in acknowledgment of Father Diamond's wit, but Larry and Mary-Margaret looked at him askance. What on earth is he on about? Mary-Margaret asked herself, momentarily distracted. Hanging on to an oasis?

I'll pop along in any case, said Mrs. Armitage. It won't be any trouble.

It had been weird in the church when Mary-Margaret got there that morning. There was only Father Diamond and everything so quiet and so empty, as if the stripping of the altars had taken something with it, some essential thing that Mary-Margaret could not name. She felt all shivery. She couldn't even look at the open tabernacle. It was like looking at something shameful, someone naked, a dead person in the road. But now that the others—Seamus too, all hands on deck—were there and busying about with dustpans and with bin bags, she felt a little better. She wondered if they could hear the beating of her heart.

Father Diamond and Seamus brought the ladder in (where had they hidden it before?) and began their widdershins progress round the church. They worked systematically, starting at the door, carrying the ladder between them. In front of each image they halted and the priest climbed up, while Seamus steadied him. Mary-Margaret watched them out of the corner of her eye. Stealth and cunning. That's what it took. Mary-Margaret was no one's fool.

The statue of St. Joseph first. Then the big painting of a martyr. The Good Shepherd and some other dark and smudgy paintings of unlabeled saints. When Larry Armitage noticed what was happening, he hurried over to collect the fallen cloths. Mrs. Armitage joined him with her duster. They moved to the first chapel. And then to the Chapel of the Holy Souls. Mary-Margaret averted her face from them while they were there. She pretended to tidy up the trays of cards and pamphlets by the door, as if she had no interest whatsoever in the unveiled crucifix. Stealth and cunning, she reminded herself. She'd wait until they were distracted by the difficulty of unwrapping the big cross that hung over the high altar. Meanwhile she held her breath.

Oh God, what could be taking them so long? There was the sound of rushing wind. Mary-Margaret stopped her ears against it but it was just as loud. Be a love and put the kettle on, Mrs. Armitage called down to her from the entrance to the chapel. So, had they done it then at last? Only say the word, she prayed, my dear, my darling, my sweetheart and my Savior, get on and say the word, O God. I'll do that, she shouted back to Mrs. Armitage. Be there in a tick.

Slowly, casually, as one with absolutely no care in the

world and no thought in her mind other than the brewing of the tea, Mary-Margaret strolled up the side aisle past the chapel. At its entrance she stopped. Mrs. Armitage and the others were clustered in the sanctuary round the ladder, on the top rung of which Father Diamond stood and stretched precariously. They paid her no attention. She went in. She knelt. Could her heart literally burst? She looked up into the beautiful and suffering face of her tormented God. I'm here, she whispered. And I'm ready. Silent and unmoving, the plaster face gazed down. The painted eyes remained unblinking. The drops of blood upon His side and on His hands, His feet, His wounded head stayed as they were, dull red, solidified.

Mary-Margaret stood up. She climbed the step up to the altar. She reached for the foot of the crucifix and pressed her hand against it. I'm sorry it took so long, she said. Forgive me. But I'm here now. And I'm all ears. And I really love you.

Still the face stared down. His lips stayed sealed. If he saw her standing at his feet and weeping, he gave her no sign. Where have you got to, Mary-Margaret? Mrs. Armitage was calling.

I suppose you expect me to paint some bunnies or some baby chicks on these? Felix had positioned the first of his hard-boiled eggs in the specially designed egg clamp from the Easter painting kit that came out once a year. He was considering it with care and a poised paintbrush. His mother wasn't listening. Almonds, she said. A hundred grams. Ground. And pistachios.

Mum! Listen up! Did you hear my question? Do you want rabbits, or what?

Sorry, darling. I am listening. Rabbits? Well, what would you like to paint? Rabbits are conventional.

Spiders, Felix said. And tiggy hogs. I could do them with felt pen. These paints are a bit old now, they're all dry and crumbly.

Spiders would be a change, most certainly. Whatever you want, Felix. Stella looked down at the back of his bent head and stopped herself from kissing the bare nape of his neck. The paints will probably be all right, though, when they're mixed with water.

Felix stopped to watch Stella separate four eggs. In marble halls as white as milk, he quoted. Lined with a skin as soft as . . . How do you say this word, Mum—s-i-l-k?

Silk, she said.

What do cows drink?

Milk.

No, they don't! Everybody falls for that, it's silly. Can I do the whisking? I wish you were making chocolate cake.

This cake will be green, she said, or green-flecked. I'll make a chocolate one for you next Sunday. You probably wouldn't want to have a chocolate cake and a chocolate egg tomorrow.

Actually I would. But a cake next Sunday would be nice as well. Thank you. Are these stiff enough?

Perfect!

Stella folded the beaten whites into her mixture. Felix brushed water into yellow paint and watched the color come to life. I'll do one with chickens, he said. Do you remember when we tried to blow the eggs? Disgusting!

Maybe I'll do a dragon on this one. It could be a dragon hatching. Here be dragons. You know, when people believed the earth was flat, did they think that if they got to the end they would actually fall off?

I'm not sure what they thought. I suppose for them the ends of the earth were so remote they could not be imagined. That's why they marked their maps: terra incognita. The unknown land. Where there might be dragons.

But they must have had some sort of picture in their heads, Felix protested. Like, if they thought the earth was really flat, flat as a board, did they think that the water from the oceans just poured off? Or did they think that something kept the water on? A wall perhaps? Were they afraid that if they steered off course in their little boats, read the stars wrong or whatever, they might suddenly find themselves sailing off the edge into outer space?

Stella put the cake into the oven and turned to look at her son. I wonder if they were less literal-minded than we are today, she said. Whether they believed what they had heard and didn't stop to scrutinize the details. I mean, entirely sane and reasonable people believed all sorts of things that we find ludicrous. Pliny, for instance, the Elder, I think, described a one-legged tribe who stood on their shoulders and used their feet as shelter from the rain. Leonardo da Vinci drew unicorns. To people in the olden days, the world must have seemed so new and strange, so full of surprises, that another one or two, however improbable, hardly made a difference. We've lost that sense of wonder, but we've kept the same credulity in some ways. We accept all sorts of things on other people's say-so. The way the Internet works, or that there was water once on Mars.

Was there? Really?

Come to think of it, I'm not completely sure. It was something I read recently, I can't remember where. So, you see? I could believe that it was true and tell you, then you would believe it too, but neither of us would ever see the proof.

But we could be wrong, because we haven't seen the proof.

Yes of course—we could be wrong. That's the hazard of belief. But you can't check every single thing that you believe independently, for yourself. A whole lifetime would be too short for that.

That's why I like science. It lets you look at one thing closely: wood lice.

Yes, but even then there will always be terra incognita, undiscovered facts about a wood louse. For example, scientists the other day observed that rooks can make hooks out of wire. Once upon a time, toolmaking was one of the things that defined being human. But now we know that birds can make them too. And yet you would have thought that, after living with them for thousands of years, we'd know all there was to know about rooks and crows. Imagine. If that's what a bird brain is capable of, what might a whale do, or even a wood louse?

A whale would find it hard to make a hook. It couldn't bend the wire with its flippers.

That is a fair point. Now, that cake will be done in half an hour. Will you come and help me with the flowers?

If I have to, Felix said. I'll just paint a whale on this.

*

Alice Armitage wondered where Mary-Margaret had gone. There was no sign of her anywhere and the kettle had not been boiled. She must have rushed off suddenly. Daft as a brush, that girl, she said. See you later, Father.

Mary-Margaret could not have said how she got home. She remembered nothing between stumbling out of the chapel and arriving at the flat, where she found Fidelma in her usual place beside the window.

Better weather today, Fidelma said. Sunshine, maybe. You were up betimes, this morning?

Yes.

Fidelma looked sharply at her daughter. Is something wrong?

No.

That's good. I like it when it's clear enough to see across the city.

Fidelma against the window was a vast black stain. Mary-Margaret stared at her. A brooding hulk, a great black monster, a creature straight from hell. A hag in the disguise of a woman, a woman buried in rotten flesh, dressed in a black skirt and black turtleneck, dirty slippers on her swollen feet. Her legs were pillars of lard, dimpled as if by fondling fingers. She sat with them wide apart. Between them was a dark place, evil. Mary-Margaret shuddered with disgust. This foul thing was her mother. It stank of woman, wickedness and sweat. Its fingers and its teeth were stained. And it dared to smile? Its mouth opened and said something about food. This abomination, whose mouth was full of bleeding flesh, whose body had been host to filth and wickedness. This whore of Babylon.

Then Mary-Margaret knew. She heard a voice, and it

told her clearly: behold, you were conceived in sin. So clear the voice that Mary-Margaret turned to see who else was in the room. There was no one but Fidelma. The mother who had sinned. And smeared her blackness on her daughter. A daughter who now understood exactly what she had to do. I was blind but now I see; how could I have doubted you, my Lord?

Left alone in the church, Father Diamond rehearsed the day. It was almost one o'clock. He could have a break for a couple of hours. Perhaps he ought to get himself some lunch? Technically, Lent was over; he could have some cheese or a ham sandwich. But, after forty days of abstinence, the thought of fat or flesh made him a little queasy. He imagined the feeling on his tongue, the sliminess and grease. No, he wasn't that hungry. All he seemed to want these days were thin things, sharp things: black coffee, lime juice, Marmite, olives.

The Easter vigil was at eight o'clock. He ran through it in his mind. The high point of the year, the great celebratory Easter Eucharist, source and summit of life, validation of the cross and triumph over death, the victory of light. Thine be the glory, risen, conquering Son. It was a complex service. The blessing of the fire, the service of light, the lighting of the paschal candle, the blessing of water, the renewal of baptismal promises, the Easter Proclamation, the nine Scripture readings, the Gloria, the bells. Christ the morning star, who came back from the dead. Genesis, Exodus, Isaiah, Ezekiel: the Creation, the parting of the sea, Abraham and Isaac. Take now thy son, thine only son, whom thou lovest, even Isaac, into the land of Moriah, upon one of the mountains which I will tell thee of. . . . And Abraham stretched forth his hand, and took the knife . . .

Father Diamond missed Father O'Connor more than ever. It had been cruel of him, really, to prolong his sabbatical over Easter. Normally, it would be Father O'Connor who had charge of the ceremonies, while Father Diamond assisted. Although he would have help tonight—the neighboring parish had very generously lent him a spare Jesuit— it was not the same. As he was acting parish priest, the responsibility today was Father Diamond's. From where he was, worn-out and full of doubt, the twenty-four hours to come were like the highest mountain and he a traveler who, with no way round, was made to climb it. Cliffs of fall, frightful, sheer, no-man-fathomed. Hold them cheap may who ne'er hung there. It was a long and lonely climb.

Father Diamond walked slowly round the church, checking every detail. The special candlestick was there, the stoup was full of water. Why was he so bleak, on this day of all days? Where was the leap of the heart, the lift of the soul he ought to feel, in the love of the risen Lord who turned mourning into dancing?

He went into the sacristy and began to rinse out the vases which had been unused during Lent except for the Fourth Sunday. There was some consolation in the thought of flowers again. In the thought of seeing Stella. Stella admirabilis, lady of silences, star of the sea. He dried the vases and placed them ready for her by the sink. Then, having checked that the outside door to the sacristy was locked, he went back into the church, knelt for a few min-

utes at the altar, made the sign of the cross and let himself
out by the main door, which he also locked.

Mary-Margaret, back in the flat, sat down to eat beef burg-
ers and potato wedges with her mother. She was safe if she
kept her face turned from Fidelma's. She knew that if she
looked straight at her, what might seem like dribbles of red
ketchup on her mother's lips would in reality be blood. She
looked out of the window instead, at the block opposite,
at the immense spread of London, the intimation of green
hills. What's up? Fidelma asked, but Mary-Margaret said
nothing.

When they had finished eating, Mary-Margaret cleared
away the meal and collected what she needed from the
kitchen. That morning she had folded the dress into a bag
with her First Communion veil. The crucial thing was to
find Shamso. It occurred to her she might need rope. Where
would she get that? There was nothing in the flat except
some worms of string tangled in the jumble of a drawer.
If her dressing gown had a sash, then that might do, but
it fastened with a zip. Her mother did not have a dressing
gown as far as she knew; she simply pulled an old gray car-
digan over her nightdress of a morning, if the weather was
particularly cold. Neither woman owned a belt. Even in her
present state of mind, the thought of a belt belonging to her
mother made Mary-Margaret smile. It would look like the
understrap of an elephant's saddle.

She went back into the living room. Fidelma was smok-
ing a cigarette. Are you making tea? she asked.

I wasn't going to, Mary-Margaret said, still looking away. But I will if you want.

That would be nice. Have you got toothache?

No. Where do you get rope?

Rope?

Rope. Or cord. You know.

What do you want rope for?

Nothing, Mary-Margaret said.

Fidelma watched her go back into the kitchen. Ever since her teens, Mary-Margaret had had a most peculiar gait. She did not simply put one foot in front of the other, as ordinary people did, but swayed from side to side with every step, like a stamping duck, if there was such a thing. Even in the small confines of this space her daughter hustled and bustled. What was she going on about, these cords and rope? Not some grisly form of penance, Fidelma hoped.

They used to say the priest wore a thorny rope next to his skin. The priest who ruled over the house of the sisters in the city. It was the only possible explanation for his temper. When it scratched his soft belly beyond bearing, he'd lash out at the nearest young one with his hand or tongue. At least he never lashed out with the thing itself. Fidelma shuddered. Think of it, a knotted cord, stiff with blood and the dirt of his body, black with it, like the unwashed clothes of poor men who walked the road. Not a pretty sight. Well so, he had the decency to keep it under wraps, although there were those who said he showed more of himself than any man, let alone a man who thought of himself as holy, was right to do. But never to Fidelma. Probably she was too spiny, too much of a thorn in the flesh herself, thank God. That's what a sister had once called her. A thorn in the flesh. It was the soft ones, the pretty ones, the ones with petal mouths and fat white cheeks who got the worst of it, in those days. Fidelma was fast enough to dodge the fumbling hands. She remembered her young self. A thin and whippy girl, dark-eyed and scornful, with a mouth the sisters accused of insolence. Though sweet enough to those who kissed it.

But even that lithe and darting girl had not been quick enough to skip away from the falling lash. Nobody was. Impartially, impersonally, the sisters doled out the punishment of beating. Well, to be fair, not all the sisters. There were one or two who would look on with pitying eyes while their sisters in Christ administered beatings to the backsides of young children, and would afterward attempt to soften the blows with a secret lump of sugar or a twist of jam and bread.

No, it would not be fair to tar them all with the same brush. Nor the priests neither. They were not all of them devils with hands ready to thrust down the knickers of young girls or cocks twitching at the sight of little boys. But some. And all of them, it seemed, turned a blind eye to the beatings and to the worse thing the sisters did.

Fidelma would not let herself think back to that. Instead she contemplated rope. In all the world was there a smell more lovely than the smell of tarry rope salt-steeped and drying in the sun? Those fat coils like serpents happily asleep, on the jetty of the harbor, in the bottom of fishing boats.

Please God, I hope he did not drown. I hope he coils his ropes still, and the drops of cold seawater still fly off them like scattered diamonds as he does.

Here's your tea, Mary-Margaret said, putting the cup beside her. I'm off out now for a while. I'll see you later, I suppose.

Well, I suppose so too, Fidelma said. You've nowhere else to come back to, I don't suppose. But enjoy your outing. And take care of yourself now, won't you?

A Saturday afternoon. Where would the Abdis be? Mary-Margaret knocked on their front door. No answer. At the shops, perhaps? She pressed the button for the lift and waited impatiently. It was almost four o'clock. She did not have much time. The lift heaved noisily upward and the door opened. A mosaic of vomit in one corner, the usual flotsam of crisp packets and sweet wrappers, the scent of stale pee. It took an age to jerk its way back down. There were children in the playground, but no Abdis. Dear God, where would they be? They never went far afield; Mrs. Abdi couldn't manage. The park? Mary-Margaret remembered Shamso quacking. Of course. Stupid her. Why hadn't she thought of that before?

She walked as fast as she could, half-stumbling, half-trotting down Falcon Road. The afternoon was bright and clear, a little breezy. There were white flowers on the trees in the park. A boy and his father were flying a blue kite. Out of breath, Mary-Margaret hurried to the pond. And was rewarded. There, by the edge of the water, were Hodan and Faduma, Bahdoon, Sagal and Shamso. Hodan was clutching Shamso round the waist as he leaned forward to cast his broken bread into the water. Even from a distance, Mary-Margaret could hear the noise that he was making.

She slowed down. All at once she sensed a need for caution. As the eldest, Hodan was protective. Mary-Margaret stopped and fumbled for the purse in her shoulder bag. Oh! That was a narrow squeak; a good thing she had wrapped it in a tea towel. She had a five-pound note and four pounds sixty-something in loose change. More than enough, she thought.

She strolled casually toward the children. Bahdoon, shaking crumbs out of a plastic bag which he had grabbed from Sagal, saw her first. She waved. Bahdoon said something to the others, who turned round. Hi, gang, Mary-Margaret said. How are you? Hi, Shamso.

Shamso smiled his pearly smile and ran to her. She knew what he would look for. She let him search the pockets of her fleece, though she kept her bag well out of reach. Her pockets were empty but for a set of keys and some tissues.

No sweeties! I'm sorry, Shamso. His face fell. But you could have an ice cream. Would you like that, kids? Ice cream, ice cream, the children chorused, jumping up and down.

I saw a van by the gate into the park, she said to Hodan, indicating the direction from which she'd come. Why don't you go and get them and leave Shamso here with me? He'll get tired if you make him walk the whole way there and back, and he'll slow you down. She held out the five-pound note.

Hodan's eyes widened with surprise. But she took the

money, said something in her own language to the others, bent to give Shamso an instruction, grabbed Sagal by the hand and scampered off, with Bahdoon and Faduma on her tail.

As soon as they were gone, Mary-Margaret picked Shamso up and ran as fast as she could toward the gate in the opposite direction. Shamso, maybe thinking this was a new game she was playing, laughed and held on tight. But he was a deadweight and soon began to squirm. Mary-Margaret put him down and tried to catch her breath. At once he ran away and she had to chase after him across the grass. How could so small a person be so quick?

This was a difficulty unforeseen. He was too heavy to carry all the way but he was in no mood to walk obediently beside her. At the best of times, progress with him was very slow. She seized his hand and pulled him. He resisted. Chocolate, she said. Good boy. Let's go and buy some sweeties.

Even so, she had to tug him and he protested loudly. It felt like a long way, alternately carrying and cajoling him while he yelled. Parents walking with their children watched her pass, giving her commiserating or condemning looks. Oh bless, said a mother with a small crowd in tow. Someone needs his nap now, don't he!

At the Sun Gate Mary-Margaret came to a halt. Good boy, she said again. Now she reached into her bag for the leftover packet of chocolate fingers she had taken from the kitchen. Shamso cheered up at the sight. She unwrapped the packet, tearing clumsily at the plastic, ripping the inner cardboard. Good boy. She pushed a biscuit into his mouth.

Now that he was quieter, their way was easier, especially

as the main shopping street was busy with people profiting from the long weekend. Mary-Margaret tried to look like one of them, strolling with her little son, glancing into windows. As a matter of fact there was something she had to buy, she said to Shamso.

We don't do rope, a woman said, in a shop called Cuisinalia. We do have culinary string. She showed Mary-Margaret a cone of string wrapped round a metal spindle. It cost £11.99 and looked too thin to tie up anything larger than a duckling.

The flower shop, the shop with handbags that cost more than Mary-Margaret had to spend in a whole year, the shop with the posh cheese, Oxfam and the Mind shop—they were no good either. Would the butcher give her something? No harm in asking. She sometimes bought mince and sausages from him, cheaper than the supermarket.

Cord, love? D'you mean trussing string? Doing a rolled joint, are you? Well, I don't sell it, but I'll let you have a bit. He cut off a twelve-inch length, and Mary-Margaret thanked him.

Too bad. She'd just have to do without. Time was ticking away fast. Shamso, still pacified with biscuits, was cooperative enough at the moment but she couldn't bank on him staying like that for long. She lifted him up again and headed for the Sacred Heart.

Fate was on her side. On the corner of a residential street, between the main road and the church, was a shop that Mary-Margaret had ignored in the past, knowing it had nothing for her. There were clay pots in the window and a small tree on the doorstep with narrow, silvery leaves; inside, watering cans and decorative labels, wooden clogs and packets of seed. She wasn't sure what kind of shop it was but she saw that each pot in the window held a ball of thick, green string.

How much is the string? she asked. And is it strong enough?

The gardening twine, you mean? And strong enough for what? It all depends, of course. The man in the shop laughed. How long *is* a piece of string? You may well ask. And it's £3.99 to a pretty face like yours. Here, watch it, son, he added, retrieving a glass bowl from Shamso.

Mary-Margaret gave him the pound coins and put the penny change into the box for muscular dystrophy beside the till. On second thoughts she put the rest of her coins into the box as well. To rid herself of all earthly encumbrance was a fitting start and gave her lightness in her being. Ta, the shopkeeper said. Do you need a bag?

There was no one in the forecourt of the church. Mary-Margaret tried the main door even though she knew it would be locked. Grabbing Shamso by the wrist, she ran round the corner to the sacristy door, which she opened with the key she had removed on Thursday.

In the draft from the opening door a row of surplices hanging on a rail stirred slightly, as if their ghostly wearers had felt the sudden chill. Black cassocks hung from pegs along the wall like bodies left to swing from gibbets, redolent of damp and mildew. There was the breath of incense too, and dust, and the stale tang of old washcloths rolled and left to fester in the sink. A neat line of clean vases and two sets of vestments beautifully laid out. The best vestments, Mary-Margaret noted, white silk stiff with gold, gold-tasseled, gold-embroidered lilies, sacred clothes scented with cedarwood, ready for a bridegroom, fit for feast days, still as waiting shrouds. A clock ticked loudly on the wall.

Before she could stop him, Shamso caught the edge of the nearer chasuble and pulled. The whole precisely folded assemblage slid with the silk on which it had been laid straight onto the floor. Jesus, Mary and Joseph! Mary-Margaret swore. She felt like smacking Shamso. What a waste of precious time to be laying out the lot again in such a way that Father Diamond wouldn't see the difference. She tried as best as she could. Shamso had left a big smear of chocolate on the silk. She wet a corner of a washcloth and dabbed at the mess but only made it worse. Oh help, she said to Shamso, feeling flustered. He was playing hide-and-seek by himself between the surplices, leaving his fingerprints on them as well.

She left him to it while she changed. She couldn't take off all her normal clothes, not there, not in the sacristy, so she only removed her fleece and knitted top. The dress was a bit too tight, quite a bit in fact, but it was lovely— a shiny fabric overlaid with lace, long sleeves with pearly buttons—and in any case they had only had one in the shop. She wriggled it over her head, pushed her arms into the sleeves and got completely stuck. Shamso, hearing her cry of fright, looked out from his surplice tent and laughed. Extricating herself somehow, Mary-Margaret tried again, leaving her arms out, tugging hard. Something tore, but she paid no notice. Her heart was beating so wildly now she thought she might black out. But mercifully then she heard the voice again, reassuring, calming her, telling her not to be afraid. The white folds of the dress slid into place. Taking a deep breath, Mary-Margaret put on the veil, scooped Shamso out of the hanging robes and unlatched the connecting door into the church.

Stella, Felix and Father Diamond converged on the path by the side of the church. Stella and her son were almost invisible behind the branches of mimosa, the roses and the green fronds they both carried. Hello, Felix culpa, Father Diamond said, in a greeting that Felix could construe but did not understand; so Birnam Wood has come to Dunsinane!

There is more to carry, Stella said. We have cherry blossom, but no broom. And lilies. They are in the car.

I'll fetch them, Father Diamond said. First let me open the door. Stella had a smudge of yellow pollen like gold dust on her cheek; she was looking very beautiful, Father Diamond thought.

He opened the door, held it to let Stella and Felix pass, and set off down the path toward the car. Stella, having laid her flowers on the counter by the sink, went after him, telling Felix she would be back in a second. Felix, alone in the sacristy, admired the floating whiteness of the robes and the embroidery on the priest's clothes, the entwined flowers and leaves, the contrast with the austerity of the black ones hanging from their hooks. He had been in this place before, with Stella, but seldom; he enjoyed the sense of trespass and of privilege it brought him. Through the open door daylight poured in; the air at once had filled with the scent of flowers.

In the church Mary-Margaret had made her preparations. She had to keep an eye on Shamso all the time, in case he did more damage, but he, awed perhaps by the silence and the space, the dimness broken by pools of color spilled by sunlight through stained glass, the lifelike figures, stayed close to her and made no sound. She was glad to see that Father Diamond had not yet prepared the altar. There was nothing on it but a linen cloth.

Come, Shamso, she said to him, my lamb. Let's go and say our prayers. She led him by the hand to the Lady Chapel and held him close to her as she knelt before the statue. Blessed Mary, ever-virgin, pray for me, she said. That I will stay as pure as you, and worthy of your Son. Shamso stared solemnly at the blue-cloaked lady and was quiet. Mary-Margaret struggled to her feet, still clasping him. She had one more prayer and one last hope, before she did the thing she had to do.

There He was, in the Chapel of the Holy Souls. Ah, she breathed. I know that my Redeemer lives, who died for me, and for my mother's sins. She gazed up through the darkness at His sorrowful face. She ached to touch it, to kiss it, to set her mouth on His, to wipe away His tears. He said nothing, and His eyes remained downcast, but Mary-Margaret felt a sudden rush of strength, a warm rush that gave her such a sense of certainty and purpose that she no longer had the slightest doubt. And with that pulsing heat another feeling. One that flowed from a secret part of her, an excitement that was also languorous, that made her think of stretching out on soft grass in hot sunshine, looking into loving eyes, an unimaginably gentle hand, a fluttering of yet unopened wings inside her.

I love you, she said out loud. And she hugged Shamso closely, pressing her lips to his yielding cheek.

Putting the child down, she took one of the candlesticks from the foot of the cross and beckoned him to follow her to the high altar.

Alice Armitage, hurrying toward church, trying to remember if Father D had said five or half past, running through the mental list of what she had to do, wondered why she felt uneasy. It was an anxiety that stayed just out of sight, a troubling shadow in the outer field of vision, a sense of foreboding that was strange to her, this most rational of women. It must be that dream I had last night, she said, or a touch of gippy tummy; silly nonsense, but even so, as she walked at her brisk pace down Riverside Crescent, she found herself saying over and over again: please keep him safe, O Lord, O Lord, please keep him safe.

On a low shelf in the sacristy were two china bowls, ordinary kitchen bowls, half-filled with incense. One was labeled ROSE, the other MYRRH. Felix picked out a crystal of the myrrh. It had no scent in his fingers so he supposed it must need fire. He replaced it quickly when he heard returning footsteps on the gravel path—his mother's or the priest's. Then he heard the scream. He did not stop to think. It was a high-pitched scream, a baby's, or a cat's, a cry of complete terror. He wrenched at the latch of the connecting door and hurtled through into the church.

A black child on the whiteness of the altar, lit by a single candle, struggling against green ropes. A child howling. A veiled figure robed in white, facing the cross, back to the body of the church, one arm upraised, the candle's flame reflected in a knife blade. The knife was poised. Stop, cried Felix, rushing to seize the lifted arm. And Mary-Margaret, startled by the sound and frightened, jerked round and swung the knife out wildly, catching Felix in the neck.

Stella, arriving at the door, saw the spout of red. She flung herself at Felix and caught him as he fell, the blood still pulsing, his eyes rolling backward in his head. Father Diamond, close behind, was frozen. Get something to stanch it, Stella ordered, clearly, and not shouting. He heard her through the noise of the shrieking woman and the wailing baby. The first thing to hand in the sacristy was his embroidered stole; he grabbed it and ran to Stella.

Alice Armitage was perturbed to find the main door locked. There were only three hours to go; Father Diamond was cutting it a bit fine, surely? Arranging flowers properly took time. She went round to the side door. It was open. There were terrible sounds inside. The sight that met her was unreal, a nightmare, or a vision: Stella Morrison kneeling by the altar with a child in her arms, both of them drenched in a red so bright and clear it could not be anything but innocent; Father Diamond kneeling by her; Mary-Margaret O'Reilly stock-still beside them, making rhythmic, choking, high-pitched sounds like a soul in torment, or a tortured dog. And, lashed onto the altar, a small child. A sacrifice, a deposition, a pietà, a hideous sacrilege.

Alice kept her head. Immediately she found her mobile

in her handbag and keyed in 999. Ambulance, she said. And the police. She doubled back into the sacristy to get an altar cloth from the chest there, folded it and crouched down next to Stella to help put pressure on the wound. Felix was not conscious. Alice only knew the boy by sight. She couldn't remember his name. You'll be okay, sweetheart, she kept saying. Hang on in there, love. Father Diamond, in the way now, stood up and for the first time took in Shamso. The child had nothing on except a nappy. Three lots of green cord bound him to the altar, at his ankles, thighs and chest. The knots were tight and difficult for fumbling fingers to undo. After an eternity of struggle, Father Diamond gathered the sobbing child into his arms. Alice instructed him to open the main door to save the paramedics time.

They took Felix and Stella. The police, arriving minutes later, tried without success to get some sense out of Mary-Margaret and finally led her away. Others came for Shamso. Screeching sirens intensified the horror. Neither the priest nor Mrs. Armitage could identify the child, and for a moment Father Diamond was reluctant to surrender the warm and trusting weight of him into the policeman's arms. More police were promised; scenes of crime and so on, but for a few minutes Alice Armitage and Father Diamond were on their own. They faced each other, blood spattered on the bloodstained sanctuary, and there was nothing they could say. Racked, both of them, with heaving sobs, they stumbled into one another's arms and clung there, until more policemen came.

*

Fading daylight giving way to the blaze of streetlamps and neon-bright stairwells; lights flaring across South London, in cars, in windows; buildings making frames of black. Fidelma stopped in her own darkness for a while, watching the lights flash on, strings of lights like precious stones. Was Mary-Margaret intending to make a habit of staying out till late, without saying where she was going or when she was coming back? Fidelma was not particularly worried. Mary-Margaret was an adult now; responsible, up to a point, able to look after herself, to some extent. The accident—the broken head—well, that was a one-off surely; no one could be so careless or unlucky as to incur a second hospital admission within a fortnight or thereabouts. Although it was true, of course, that lightning could strike twice. But not very likely all the same.

That Mary-Margaret might have a secret life struck Fidelma as absurd. She was an open book, that girl—concerned solely with God and shopping. And neither of them especially perilous pursuits, in the usual way of things, the foreseeable run of the world. No, the probable explanation was that she had gone off somewhere with the baby she treated like a doll, and would be back in time for the fish cakes that she knew her mother would be cooking. And in the meantime her mother was not discontent to stay in her roosting place by the window, with her cigarettes and a tube of spring-onion-flavored Pringles. These thin wafers of green-flecked potato nestled one into the next so satisfactorily, with the elegance of a snake's backbone or the scales of a fish. And broke so crisply on the tongue, blessing it with an aftertaste of salt and fat.

✳

Thousands of miles away, Camilla Morrison slept easily on her mattress in a room with a bamboo-slatted floor, lullabied by tree frogs and the softness of a warm wind full of rain. In a pub in Much Wenlock her brother Barnaby held the hand of the girl he loved and decided not to go home till tomorrow. He texted his mother with his change of plans and turned off his telephone. Beginning the climb into the air in a first-class cabin above the Atlantic Ocean, Rufus Morrison caught on his skin the scent of the woman whose bed he had left that afternoon. He would not share that bed again, nor would the woman want him to; for both of them it had been an insignificant encounter. Sergeant Fraser Armitage, in Musa Qala, checked his watch and reminded the boys to get an early night. It might be Easter Sunday in the morning but that made no difference here. It would be their last patrol. They were warned against becoming demob happy. Much closer to St. Elizabeth's Hospital, but further away from home, Kiti Mendoza and her Auntie Rita were filling spring-roll wrappers with shredded pork and bean sprouts, ready to be fried tomorrow. And, in a windowless room in St. Elizabeth's, Father Diamond found Stella.

They don't want me there, she said. They said it would be better if I waited here. She did not look surprised to see him.

I've got your car keys, he said. How is he? He had left his church still buzzing with police officers and their clamor of witnesses and statements, cordoned areas, padlocks and guards. They had wanted him to stay but he had insisted on going to Stella; anything else would have to wait, he told them, with a new firmness of purpose. He had picked up her keys from where she had left them by the flowers and had checked her car was locked. On an impulse he also picked up a stem of cherry blossom.

The corridors of the hospital were deathly familiar to him; their chemical reek; the harsh lighting, the sad notices on pinboards offering advice or invitations to buy raffle tickets. Everybody shuffling or hurrying through those passages seemed portentous in a way they would not in an ordinary place, as if each had a secret, either as sufferer, survivor or as healer, or were bearing occult knowledge. Father Diamond had noticed this before, as an observer merely. Tonight he shared in their importance, was bonded to the people in the corridors by the blood of a child and the pain of a suffering mother. He carried something in his heart that had more weight than anything he had known before.

They had told him where to go at A & E reception but, as in a nightmare, he kept losing his way in this building he knew so well, blundering through the wrong sets of plastic swinging doors. When, at last, he came to Stella, the reality of the situation hit him with such force he had to hold on to the lintel of the door. Felix's blood was still drying on her jeans and her blue shirt. He gave her the stem of blossom, which she took without a word.

Would you like me to pray with you? Father Diamond asked her, without much hope.

Not really, Stella answered. At least, not with me, out loud. But I would like you to pray, please, if you can.

She had been standing when he arrived and now sat

down on one of the plastic chairs lined up against the wall. He took the chair beside it and held out his hand. She took and held it. Her hand was very cold. He saw that she was shivering; she had nothing with her. He took off his black jacket and put it round her shoulders. In silence he prayed, and in silence they waited for a time that was beyond time, too fast and too slow, a lifetime and one beat of a heart. Then the door was opened cautiously and a young man in light blue scrubs came in. Felix's mum? he asked. I'm so very sorry.

Silence fell on them again for an eternal moment before the doctor began to talk about blood loss and blood pressure, a spate of words that bounced off the depths of Stella's incomprehending grief like hailstones off a frozen lake. She was as pale as death herself. She rose slowly and let go her grip on Father Diamond's hand, giving hers instead to the doctor. Thank you for trying so hard, she said. May I see him now?

Through a cloud so thick it was near blindness Father Diamond watched Stella and the doctor go, leaving him behind. Two slight figures dressed in blue, both sprayed with blood, his own jacket still round Stella's shoulders, slipping; blue, and black, and red now drying to the rust of dying petals. White blossom where Stella had left it, on the floor. Terrible words came to him in the shattered silence. Blessed are the barren, and the wombs that never bear, and the breasts that never gave suck. For if the end of loving is sorrow beyond bearing, is it not better from the first to forswear love?

*

The facts were not in question. Witnesses saw to that. Interpretation was the point. Dr. Azin Qureshi peered at the words of his report, backlit on a screen, as if by searching he could make them shift apart to reveal a secret subtext or a second meaning. But, however hard he looked, they stayed stubbornly unmoving, merciless and stark. One dead child, another child abducted; that child the victim of attempted murder.

Dr. Qureshi had been on call that Saturday. Requests for duty doctors to attend the recently arrested were routine, but this time the sergeant who summoned him talked about serious charges and a prisoner in urgent need. Dr. Qureshi set aside his supper and made haste.

It was clear at once that the woman being held was in no state to be questioned. Nor could she be left in a police cell overnight. She was mute, shaking, wearing a bloodstained wedding dress and in deep shock. Dr. Qureshi arranged for her admittance to the secure unit at St. Elizabeth's; risk of self-harm, he warned. Keep watch.

He had nothing more to do with her until after the bank holiday. Then, because of the gravity of the case and because he was the senior consultant, he formally accepted her as a patient. At the time of her admittance, he knew only she had been taken into custody after the injury of a child. Neither he nor the police knew then that the child was dead.

As a matter of course, a child's death would not necessarily make front-page news. But this child was the son of a member of the Shadow Cabinet, and mortally wounded in a church. The holiday weekend held back reporting for a day, but there was no stopping it after that. Kiti Mendoza played an early part, before the full details were established. She had been met on Easter Sunday morning by a locked door, a police guard and no explanation; her immediate assumption was that the authorities were conspiring against her. All that she found, with others turning up for mass that morning, was a notice with directions to the nearest Catholic church and its service times. Father Diamond had pinned it to the main door when he got back in the early hours of the morning. Even then, he did not forget his parish duty.

He had waited at the hospital for Stella. When she returned, still with the doctor in the blue clothes, she was unnaturally calm. The young doctor had said something about GPs and sedation but neither Father Diamond nor Stella took it in. Father Diamond did understand that they were going to move the body to a nearby hospice, where it would be laid out in a cold room. A better place for the family to come to terms and say good-bye.

To come to terms? Father Diamond wondered at the doctor's wording. But then, what else could this kindly but detached professional have said of this enormity, this outrage that cried out in anger against heaven?

He drove Stella home. She opened the front door, deactivated the burglar alarm, switched on lights and led him downstairs to the kitchen, all the while apparently composed. But there were Felix's painted eggs where he had left them, on the table. Father Diamond prayed he would never hear again the sound that Stella made when she saw them.

He stayed with her until Rufus came. He told Rufus what had happened. Stella had not wanted him to telephone anybody else until Rufus had been told. But she was in agony for Camilla. How can she hear this when she is on her own? she howled. We'll find someone to break it to her gently, Father Diamond promised; if there is no one else, I will go myself. He would have promised anything if it would comfort Stella. But he knew that nothing could. He held her to him, rocked her, made consoling sounds to her, made Ovaltine, as if she were his child, knowing all the time that consolation was beyond her now. Afterward he would not speak of the hours he spent with Stella. The raw mourning of a mother should not be lightly told.

Children get stabbed all the time, Azin Qureshi's wife said, when she saw the headline. That little boy in Hackney? Near the library, remember? Another random act of violence, another religious nutcase. What's the big deal here?

Was it a random act of violence? Azin Qureshi wondered. Rumors had seeped out about the child on the altar; lurid hintings at black magic and human sacrifice. One newspaper conjured up a link between this and the recent discovery of a child's torso in the Thames. Baby body parts in voodoo ritual? it asked. This tale of two children—one the son of privilege, the other of poor immigrants—unknown to one another, linked by tragedy, was irresistibly dramatic.

Shamso Abdi's mother, when interviewed through an interpreter, slightly spoiled foregone conclusions by insisting that O'Reilly would not have harmed the child. The kind white woman loved him, Mrs. Abdi said. She had not felt anxious about Shamso until late that Saturday night. As far as she was concerned, he was safe with

Mary-Margaret. Her other children had told her a confused story about ice creams but she had been too busy to pay heed. It was only after bedtime—which in her household was around eleven o'clock—that she began to worry. She had knocked on the O'Reillys' door but there had been no answer. In the three years that she had lived across the way from them, Mrs. Abdi had never seen Mary-Margaret's mother. A few nerve-racking hours had followed until, with the help of an English-speaking friend, she finally found Shamso in the care of the police. Even then she seemed to think that Mary-Margaret had been playing some strange game. Her older children, though, when questioned, claimed that Mary-Margaret had deliberately tricked them and indeed all the evidence suggested careful planning. A crumpled-up receipt for twine was in O'Reilly's bag. The owner of the garden shop remembered her and the curly-headed kid and said she was behaving oddly. Stains on garments belonging to the church indicated preparation. And, most damningly, O'Reilly was in possession of a sharpened carving knife. No spur-of-the-moment act of madness then. The police report went promptly to the Prosecution Service. Attempted murder, murder, abduction of a child. Release on bail opposed.

By then Azin Qureshi had carefully examined Mary-Margaret. She was capable of speech, but not of rational communication. However, he judged that she would be able to stand trial when the time came, and be fit to plead. She would be kept in a closed unit until then.

*

Fear is a blind bat blundering against the tight bones of her head, a fanged thing jabbing for a way out through the jelly of her eyes, a black crow spread-winged on her mouth, a tide of blood rising in her throat and promising to choke her. She cannot think, she can scarcely see, she cannot move but she can't stay still; she can only pray to die. Better far it would have been if she had not been born, nor Mary-Margaret conceived in a fishing boat beside the sea beneath the crying gulls.

Fidelma could not say who had telephoned her on Sunday morning. A social worker maybe, or a woman from the police. An efficient person with a list to tick and a hundred other things to do. Her words had whipped down the line like darts—accused, alleged, suspected—spiked words, hard words, all ending in conclusive *d*s, repeated *d*s like gunfire: wounded, tied up, dead. The darts pierced Fidelma's hearing but not her comprehension. At first she could only think there had been a serious mistake; she said so to the cool-voiced woman. But no; the woman repeated Mary-Margaret's name and checked the telephone number. That number was in Mary-Margaret's diary, with Fidelma's name, in the space where it was written: In case of emergency, please notify . . .

Fidelma closed her eyes. She could see that diary, pink, plastic-bound, embellished with the image of a kitten, its pages mainly blank. Mary-Margaret bought herself a diary every year, at the end of January, much reduced. And every year she filled in the part that called for personal details. Fidelma saw her writing, her careful, rounded hand. Every year it irked her that she did not know her blood group.

Dimly Fidelma understood that Mary-Margaret would

not be coming home that day. And nor the next it seemed, nor at any time that Miss Job-to-Do could name. You will be informed when there is information, she told Fidelma. She did not inquire if Fidelma was all right. Why should she? Fidelma was the mother of a killer and no business, in any case, of hers.

You will be informed when there is information. Meanwhile you will receive a fistful of sharp words that sting like gravel hurled. Hospital. Psychiatric. Knife wound. Child. Stabbed.

And in the meantime what will you do, you murderer's mother, walled in your own flesh, sealed in your tower, unregarded by the careless world? Will you slowly starve to death, moldering in your folds of skin? Smash through the meagerly rational aperture of window with a rolling pin? Telephone for takeaways to be dropped outside your door until there is no money left to buy them? Condemned to death; well there are worse fates, surely. Except that, in the rightful way, a woman bound to die would do so in the dawn, accompanied by jailers, hangmen, a black-clad priest with a prayer book and a look of pity in his eye. Not all alone, and step by step, as she must. And Mary-Meg, your poor suffering and murderous daughter? Doomed to die as well?

Mary-Margaret rocked herself a little, on her chair. It occurred to her that she might suck her thumb. Then she decided not to; instead she would pay attention to the doctor. She had already seen him quite a few times but until today she hadn't really been able to summon up the energy

to talk. Today she felt she'd better, because she wanted him
to stop the pills that they kept giving her to make her sleep.
She couldn't sleep, you see, because she kept seeing pictures.
To tell the truth, she saw pictures in the day as well. When
she was awake, that is. Or sleeping. Waking or sleeping it
was lovely seeing the pictures. The little boy. The little boy
in his mother's arms. Who would have known it of Mrs.
Morrison? Mrs. Morrison who probably didn't even know
Mary-Margaret's name until the day she broke her head
falling off the altar. But who had anyway been kind. Smiled
nicely, when they met. Which was not very often, as a matter of fact. But even so. Mary-Margaret had admired her.
She was very pretty. And well-dressed. And very good at
doing flowers. When she passed she left a lingering scent,
like the scent you sometimes catch when walking past posh
gardens. There is something that smells sweet in the winter. Not particularly showy—small white flowers. Anyway.
Mrs. Morrison. Who would have thought it? However
nice she was and sweet she smelled. Mrs. Stella Morrison.
Mother of God.

There were the pictures. And the sounds. So she didn't
only have to keep her eyes wide open but her ears as well, in
case He might send another message. The little boy telling
her to stop. That was God's voice in the boy, that was. She
didn't know his name. Mrs. Morrison's son. She'd never
seen him in her life. She'd seen the daughter once, but not
the little son. She could ask his name; the doctor would
know, perhaps. Perhaps he'd say it anyway, in passing, when
he was asking questions.

He did ask questions, quite a lot: how are you, how are
you feeling, are you feeling better? Are you managing to

sleep? Mary-Margaret liked him. He had a kind face. And, to be honest, he was not bad-looking. Actually, he was quite good-looking, considering. And he had lovely hands. Thin brown fingers which he brought together in a steeple, sometimes, and held beneath his chin, as if he were about to pray.

Did people of his sort pray? To elephants, maybe. She'd seen the pictures. Blue-faced gods. With lots of limbs. Nice eyes. The doctor, not the gods. Thick eyelashes, and long. Wasted on a man.

One question he asked every time: is there anything you'd like to tell me?

Yes there is, she'd say today. Yes. There is. I was never going to hurt him. God was going to stop me. And He did.

This is the church and this is the steeple. Where had she learned that rhyme? It had finger movements with it.

Here is the church, and here is the steeple;
Open the door and here are the people.
Here is the parson going upstairs,
And here he is a-saying his prayers.

Were his prayers no more than empty words flung into the wind? In the days that followed Felix's death, Father Diamond felt the gates of heaven had slammed shut or, worse, had closed on emptiness, had never led to anything at all. He tried to pray. It was his duty to say mass on Easter Sunday, but he could not do it. Instead he went to the church across the river, to which he had diverted his parishioners. A solemn mass at eleven; white vestments, candles, lilies; reminders of the ones he had abandoned in his sealed church. The risen Christ? By rising He has conquered death, the celebrant intoned, and Father Diamond, kneeling at the back with his head buried in his hands, was torn between tears and laughter.

Later, when he had completed yet another interview with the police, he got into his car and headed east. He had no destination in mind; he knew only that he wanted to be by himself and moving. After some hours he pulled off the main road at a sign which he thought said something about marshes. He must have misread it; he found he was in a run-down industrial estate. It was deserted, on a Sunday. At the edge of the estate he stopped the car, suddenly aware that he was desperately tired and thirsty and needed to relieve himself. It was late in the afternoon. Out of the confines of the car he smelled marsh water on the air, mud and something rotting cleanly, like fresh compost. A skein of geese flew overhead, clacking loudly to each other. He lifted an already loosened strand of barbed wire from the perimeter fence to make a gap that he could climb through. As he did the wire snagged on his jacket. He pulled himself free and felt it tear. A man of rags and tatters; how appropriate, he thought.

The wasteland he walked through was miry but there were marsh marigolds and water violets among the scrubby grass and windblown litter. In this abandoned place he cried out loud. Why? he asked. When Jairus's daughter died, you took her by the hand and told her to get up. Little girl, you said. Give her something to eat, you said. You called Lazarus from his tomb. You promised that not one sparrow worth two farthings would be forgotten under God. All your domestic miracles. But you let this child go. You let him bleed to death while I stood by and could do nothing. Or did nothing. As helpless as a scarecrow, as pathetic. You let him die. Why didn't you breathe your breath into his lungs before it was too late, stop him bleeding with your blood, bring him back to life?

The mothers of murdered children often say: he was an angel who did not deserve to die. No one deserves to die, least of all a child with his whole life before him. Why? His blood is on me, and if it tests my faltering faith, what will it do then to his mother? To his sister, where she mourns alone? To his father and his brother? How dare you talk of triumph over death when this sinless child is gone?

Father Diamond tramped across the marshy waste ground and heard nothing. No voice came in answer to his questions. But at least he'd voiced them; and the wind blew sea-whispers to him and at the end of this long day he would be tired enough to sleep.

It was Mrs. Armitage who recalled Fidelma. She had gone round to the church as usual on the Thursday morning after Easter because she knew it was important to keep to her routine and she wanted to give Father Diamond an invitation. I know you won't feel like a party, she told him. I don't either, to be honest. But Fraser's coming home. We want to welcome him.

Have you spoken to him?

Yes. He called, when he got to Malta. Said it was good to get the dust washed off. He'll be flying back as planned. Brize Norton. We're going to have a little get-together next Friday. Family and close friends.

Thank you, Father Diamond said. I'm honored to be asked. I'm glad he's on his way back home. And of course you have to kill the fatted calf . . . He stopped, and they did not meet each other's eyes as the unwanted implication of his words sank in.

Mrs. Armitage changed the subject. Any word of the wretched woman's mother? She's an invalid, I think.

Father Diamond had not given Mary-Margaret's mother any thought. In the distribution of their duties she was Father O'Connor's—he had never met her himself. But he did know from Father O'Connor that she was housebound.

I expect Social Services will be looking after her, he said.

I wouldn't be so sure, warned Alice Armitage. An elephant could slip through the holes in some of their nets, from what I've heard.

All right, said Father Diamond. I'll visit. Tomorrow afternoon.

Good on you, Alice said. Let me know if she's all right. If not, I can always pop up there as well—although, from the look of things and the terrible job she must have done as that loony's mother, she should be left to stew a bit, perhaps.

We'll see, said Father Diamond.

We will, said Alice Armitage. Now come and see how beautifully the floor's scrubbed up. She led him by the arm to the place by the altar where Felix had bled. It was a little lighter than its surround from her fierce scrubbing.

Well done, said Father Diamond.

But that reminds me. I nearly forgot. I haven't managed so nicely with the altar cloth. The one out of the chapel.

Father Diamond did not remember what had happened to the cloth. She reminded him: the one that the O'Reilly woman messed up when she fell. All stained with blood. No amount of bleach had worked.

Forget it, Father Diamond said. It's only a piece of cloth.

Well, we're almost back to normal, aren't we? Mrs. Armitage asked the priest. Now the police have gone?

Yes, he said, noticing for the first time how tired and strained she looked. Afterward he found she'd tucked a bunch of tulips and a teddy by the altar.

Fidelma heard the knock at the door and ignored it. It came again. A third time, harder. She blocked her ears with her hands. If she stopped listening, whoever it was would go away. On the other side of the door, Father Diamond hesitated. When there was no answer after his third try, he felt a strong sense of relief. Mrs. O'Reilly must be out. But then he remembered she was housebound. A vision came to him of people left to die alone and rot. Decomposing bodies found only when their neighbors could no longer bear the smell. Kept herself to herself, these neighbors said, explaining why they had not noticed sooner. A very private person. Mrs. O'Reilly might be dying, he thought. He had to keep on trying.

Fidelma took her hands from her ears and breathed again. The knocking had stopped. She was feeling wobbly, truth to tell, having emptied the kitchen cupboards of everything except Mary-Margaret's bottle of Irish Cream. Mary-Margaret had been gone almost a week. Or more perhaps? Fidelma was losing track of time. No one had telephoned her since Miss Jobsworth. They had no information to inform her, she supposed. Nights had followed days and she had stayed in silence, but for the thudding of her heart and the beat of panic in her veins. Over the last day or so she had begun to feel a little calmer. That might be because she wasn't hungry any longer. She was doing fine on little sips of whiskey with sweet cream.

Then she jumped out of her skin. The person at her door was now clattering the metal flap of the letter box and making a fiendish din. Mrs. O'Reilly, he was shouting. Are you there? Please let me in.

How much longer would he stay there? It made her shiver to think of a stranger lurking by her door. She waited. The voice said: if you're not well enough to speak, don't worry. I'm going to find a caretaker and a key.

Fidelma hauled herself up and waddled unsteadily to the door. She slotted the end of the security chain into its housing. She felt like the victim of a siege. Women had flung themselves from the high walls of their castles onto the rocks below—clasping their children to them—rather than confront the dishonoring intruder. There were invaders on the ramparts of her tower; she ought to see about some boiling oil. Perhaps a kitchen knife would do instead.

It took the voice a long time to return. As she had supposed. This block wasn't a luxury hotel, with receptionists ready and eager to hand out keys to anyone who asked. I'm back, the voice said, redundantly. I'm going to open the door.

The chain jerked hard. Now the door was open a few inches. Fidelma leaned against the wall beside it, with her knife. Mrs. O'Reilly? the voice inquired again. She wondered if he could hear her heart. Hell, the voice said then, to itself. And she sensed that he was testing the strength and resistance of the door.

Plywood, she thought. And thin. It wouldn't take a lot to splinter it, and then the invaders would be in.

Mrs. O'Reilly, the voice implored. Can you hear me at all? It's Alexander Diamond. Father Diamond. From the Sacred Heart.

A priest. No good would come from him. Priests— and the other black creatures of her childhood—had been crawling through her dreams. Black folds flapping, wings enclosing, darkness driving all the air away until there was only dust to breathe.

Father Diamond pushed against the chain again. Through the crack in the door he saw a figure move. Well, she was alive at least, and upright; maybe he could leave. Mrs. O'Reilly, he said again. I'm a friend of Father O'Connor.

Fidelma thought of Father O'Connor. Red-faced and blue-eyed like many men whom she had known, on the fat side, rather. Prone to covering his collar with a scarf. In his voice the softer sounds of her own past. She had never made him welcome, not exactly, but she had permitted Mary-Margaret to let him in. An insistent sort, he'd not take no for an answer anyway. He'd show up once in a while, saying: we've got to stick together, you and I. And he'd tell tall stories, drink the tea that Mary-Margaret made him, eat their biscuits, assess them both with his sharp eyes but seldom ask them questions. And, somehow, when he'd been, Fidelma would feel a slight lift of the spirits. She had not seen him in a while, though. Mary-Margaret had told her he was gone.

Father O'Connor? she said, croakily. Her own voice like a stranger's. How long was it since she had spoken? No need for words in a sealed tomb.

Yes, he said. I'm the other one. The other priest.

What do you want? she asked.

Nothing. Just to say hello. See how you are. I'd love a cup of tea, if you're making one.

There's no tea, she said.

Coffee's fine.

No coffee neither. So, you've said hello now. Hello and good-bye.

She had come closer to the gap. Through it Father Diamond could make her out, but only details; white skin, a straggle of hair, the glitter of an eye. And he could smell the acetone and sugar on her breath.

All right, he said. If you're busy. As long as there's nothing that you need. You can always call me. Here's a card.

She took the proffered slip of cardboard through the crack.

Um, nice to meet you, although briefly, Father Diamond said. I'll drop in again, shall I?

Fidelma said nothing. Pressing one eye to the gap she watched him turn away. His black back retreating. And her aloneness then pressed on her like wet earth on a grave. Wait a minute, she said.

Father Diamond could not conceal his shock at the figure leaning against the opened door. He had never seen anyone as huge. The woman was a globe of flesh, a billowing mound so shapeless it hardly looked like a human body. She was holding on to the edge of the door with one hand, and in the other a knife. He saw that she could not support herself unaided, and he did not feel threatened.

Fidelma saw a tall man in a dog collar and black jacket, wearing gold-rimmed glasses; fair-haired and bony-faced; oddly beautiful, though with something tremulous about the mouth. The black crows of the city screeched about her head. She held on tighter to the door.

What do you want? she asked again.

A glass of water? It's a close afternoon.

Well, that you could not deny, even to a dog. You'd best come in. And close the door behind you.

Mrs. O'Reilly moved slowly through a passage not much wider than herself, keeping one hand pressed to the wall and still clutching the knife. The door that led to the sitting room was open. Father Diamond followed her. His first impression was of light. On this April afternoon the sun was pouring through the plate-glass window and even from where he stood he could see miles across the city.

What an amazing view, he said. I've been in these flats before, but never as high as this.

Mrs. O'Reilly, knifeless now, came out of the adjoining kitchen with a glass of water. People like a view because it's there, she said. They don't stop to wonder what it's of.

What it's of?

Yes. Out there—office blocks and dirty streets, gas holders and train tracks—well, you wouldn't send a postcard, would you?

But, faraway . . .

Yes, she agreed. That's true. The distant hills.

May I sit down?

If you're planning to stay, she said, but she let herself sink into her chair beside the window. Father Diamond looked round. The small room was neat enough. But the woman opposite was obviously neglected. Her hair, deep brown and only slightly streaked with gray, was tangled and unwashed. Now that she was sitting he could see her legs, bare beneath the hem of her skirt, great dimpled slabs of blotchy white, forked with streaks of red; her feet in dirty slippers. He could also see she had once been lovely. Beneath the quivering layers of flesh lay the memory of bones. Her mouth was finely drawn and generous and her eyes the dark blue of deep sea or sky on summer nights, a rare and precious color.

Mary-Margaret? she asked. Her voice was shaky.

Ah. Yes. They're looking after her in hospital, I'm sure. Her doctor's asked to see me. Has he not been in touch with you?

Is it true, so?

True? Well, what have you been told?

No informative information. Except that a child is dead.

Yes. His name was Felix.

I saw it on TV, she said. But it was a tangled story. I didn't understand. I don't. Are they saying Mary-Margaret killed him?

He died from a stab wound. Your daughter had a knife. But no one saw the actual stabbing except for another little boy, and he can't say what happened.

Because he's shocked?

No. Because he's too young to speak.

Tears were running down her face. She left them unchecked. Father Diamond watched her for a while. Then he got up from his seat and went toward her. She looked at him, and her eyes were full of sorrow. Crouching down beside her, he put his arms around her. She stayed still. He smelled her smell of sweat and cigarettes and something fishy, and he held her while she sobbed.

She couldn't have meant to, she said. She wouldn't hurt a child. She's not very bright, but she is not a monster.

No, Father Diamond agreed. Did you have any sense there was something wrong—I mean, did she say anything, or seem upset?

No. A bit off-color, maybe. A bit distracted.

Well, I expect the doctor will get at the truth somehow. And she'll have a lawyer.

But they'll lock her up?

We'll see. Try not to worry. Shall I ask if you can see her?

She'd come here, you mean?

No. No, I don't think they'll let her out of the hospital just yet. I meant that you might be able to visit.

I can't do that.

Father Diamond had been kneeling beside Mrs. O'Reilly all this time. Now he got back to his feet. Why not? he asked, a little stiffly. He had not expected a flat refusal. I'd drive you there, he said. You wouldn't have to go alone.

It's not that. It's not, it's not, ah, it's difficult to explain . . .

She was crying again, so hard he knew he would get no other answer. I'll make you some tea, he said. In the kitchen he found the empty shelves. Back down he went for the second time in the fetid lift, and to the corner shop. Milk and bread and eggs. Tea and oranges. Some ham. Cigarettes, why not? He guessed the brand. Up on the nineteenth floor again, he let himself into the flat. Fidelma was quiet now. He made tea and scrambled eggs and left her with them, promising to come back.

Kiti Mendoza ate the last of Auntie Rita's leche flan. There had been a lot of food left over; Auntie Rita always cooked too much. Her friends seemed to enjoy last Sunday's picnic, even though it had lost its real purpose. But she was cross. The next day, when she heard about the child, she was mollified a little, but her curiosity was even more aroused. Something very strange and sinister was happening in that church. All this week it had been shut. But today was Saturday. She had worked an early shift. Now she had the afternoon and evening off and she was going to take another look. She didn't ask Melinda to come with her. Melinda had confessed to Auntie Rita that she wasn't really sure what she had seen all those days ago. The candle flame was wavering, she said.

Kiti, though, was confident. If the statue had not moved its eyes and bled, why would the priest have veiled it? He wanted to keep the miracle for himself, that was the thing, for himself and for the rich; he thought it was too good for common people. But everybody knows that Jesus loved common people and did not like the rich. If he were to come again, he'd come as an immigrant like her. Or an asylum seeker.

On the way to church, Kiti stopped at the print shop,

where the aspiring photographer had a Saturday job. She'd seen quite a bit of him as a result of all the goings-on. He'd taken lots of pictures and had sold some of the church—the ones with Mary-Margaret O'Reilly and the priest—when the kid was murdered. That had been a big news story. It was yesterday's story now, but Kiti expected to revive it. She thought she'd better let Zak know, so that he'd be ready.

Zak was doing some copying in the back. The shop manager shouted to him. Hiya, he said when he came out. Kiti's heart gave a little flutter. Zak was really handsome. His girlfriend, Kiti's colleague, was at a hen party in Barcelona, Kiti knew. And she also knew they were not a serious item. She told Zak her plan. But you don't really believe in all that stuff? he asked. I mean, like God and stuff. I thought you'd made it up. For a joke, yeah? A good story.

Kiti smiled at him. She knew better than to argue. Her smile found its mark. Fancy a drink tonight? Zak asked. When you're done with Jesus.

As chairman of the parish council, Major Wetherby had tentatively raised the question of reconsecration. Post sacrilege. Father Diamond supposed he should consult his bishop but something in him revolted against the idea that a child's death could make the church less holy. Indeed there was a gossamer-thin shred of consolation that his blood had spilled on sacred ground. Behind his closed eyes Father Diamond constantly saw versions of what might actually have happened in the short time he and Stella were away. It could only have taken them three or four minutes to get the flowers from her car. And then the open doors. He left Mrs. Armitage's teddy where it was as he made the preparation for the first mass he would celebrate since Maundy Thursday.

The vigil mass of the second Sunday of Easter. That morning he had been to Waitrose, where he bought grapes and salad, oatcakes, yogurt and the healthiest-looking ready meals he could find. As he did not want to cause upset, he had not chosen anything which described itself as calorie-controlled. It was a long time since he'd bought food with someone else in mind. In fact, had he done so ever? As a student he had only shopped for food to share. This imagining of another person's tastes surprised him with its pleasure.

Mrs. O'Reilly was also surprised when he knocked at her door again. I didn't think you'd come, she said.

I did tell you that I would.

I thought you were only saying.

There'll be someone round on Monday, he told her.

On the way down in the lift he tried to remember what he had eaten yesterday or the day before. Whatever his housekeeper had left for him, it must have been but, like everything else he did by rote, eating had blurred into the backdrop of his one acute and conscious feeling: a helpless ache for Stella.

The vigil mass. A week to the day since Felix died. Was there a requiem ritual to mark the passage of a week? He knew that Stella would tell the hours and the last minutes of her child. Rufus too, perhaps. A week. There would be a funeral, but not yet.

Dominica in albis, Divine Mercy Sunday. The lamb that bleedeth for the sheep. *Victor Rex, miserere.* Alleluia and Amen.

In the name of the Father and of the Son and of the Holy Spirit. Father Diamond surveyed the congregation. It was as sparse as usual, the old, familiar faces, no horror-tourists yet at the unheralded reopening of the church. Seamus was serving by his side. How strange it is that the world just carries on, Father Diamond thought, as if nothing has changed, and the truth is nothing has—except for those who loved the slaughtered child. Or the one who slaughtered him. And in himself. He would not ghoulishly affect a share of grief for someone he had barely known, or make the onlooker's empty claim to desolation. But even so, something had changed in him. He had witnessed other deaths but none that stripped the coverings from his soul.

Father Diamond was not a sentimental man. Children died and parents grieved; he had conducted funerals for some. This world heaved with pain. Why should the death of Felix Morrison make a lasting difference to him? This was not a question he would ask himself, but if he did his answer would be wordless.

A reading from the Book of the Apocalypse, Miss Daly announced.

"And when I saw him, I fell at his feet as one dead. And he laid his right hand upon me, saying, Fear not; I am the first and the last, and the living one; and I was dead, and behold, I am alive for evermore and I have the keys of death and of Hades. Write therefore the things which thou sawest, and the things which are, and the things which shall come to pass hereafter."

Father Diamond raised his head. A late entrant caught his eye; he recognized her, one of the young women who had caused so much trouble. He sighed. He was too tired to remonstrate with her again. It was all right for the moment; she was alone and had slipped quietly into a vacant pew. He bowed his head again and prayed for Stella.

As soon as the mass was over and the priest had disappeared, Kiti left her place, took a lit candle from the stand and carried it to the chapel. No one tried to stop her. The church was emptying fast. She knew she must be quick. She knelt. Listen to me, she said. I am your handmaid, Lord. She waited. She said three Our Fathers in a row. The painted eyes looked down at her, unmoved. Please hurry, she implored. Still nothing. No sign at all. No glittering eyes, no scarlet beads of blood. She began to feel very cold and very sad. Then there was a voice. Kiti couldn't swear that it came from the cross. She knew that it was meant for her but to be honest she had to say it was sort of soundless and internal. Also, she thought it spoke to her in her first language, not the blunt and unambiguous English she had learned to use now in her daily life. The words didn't come like a telephone message that could be remembered and repeated but more like a murmur, sounds heard in another room, or a light wind in the trees. They were about being brave and patient, not being frightened, about loneliness and how even loneliness would end. Later, trying to recover them, Kiti was reminded of her mother and the kinds of things her mother had said when she was unhappy as a child. At the time, nearly grown-up Kiti, this fierce and lonely girl who had not been home in years, to whom Auntie Rita was poor substitute for the family she missed, who had to face the indifference of strangers and claw her own way through this huge and alien city, who never gave way to self-pity, was suddenly surprised by tears.

Father Diamond came on the weeping girl as he was locking up the church. She was kneeling on the floor of the Chapel of the Holy Souls with a candle in her hand. She turned as she heard his steps. He saw how young she was, and pretty, with her joyful tear-streaked face. Are you all right, my dear? he asked. Is there anything I can do to help?

No thanks, she said. I'm good, I'm good.

You wouldn't like a cup of tea?

Oh, I'm going to meet my boyfriend for a drink. Thank you anyway. Maybe another time? And smiling her disarming smile, she got lightly to her feet, gave Father Diamond her burning candle, sped down the aisle and from the church.

Mary-Margaret was disappointed in the ward. The one she had been in when she broke her head was so much cozier than this, where they wouldn't let you stay in bed, the nurses were quite offhand and the food was not very nice at all. Well, it was all right sometimes—especially the lamb curry—but what she didn't like was having to eat at the same table as the others. A bigger load of creeps and weirdos you never saw in your whole life. And nothing much to do in between meetings with the doctor. Boring telly. Something called experimental art. The day before yesterday she'd said to the bloke in charge that she was thinking of a wander round the shops. Well you've got another think coming then, love, the man had said. Until then, Mary-Margaret had not known she was locked up. It was a very scary feeling. The only bit of silver lining to this particularly dark cloud was that it wouldn't last long. She'd explained that to the gorgeous doctor. And to her solicitor, who was a young woman, so young it was hardly possible she was allowed to do a proper job. She'd explained, but both of them were being really thick. Perhaps they'd never understand until they saw the risen God. And this was a worry to her. Would He come and let her out Himself? Show Himself to these two doubters? Would they recognize Him in the form of the little boy whose name she didn't know? Would she know Him, come to that? The first time round His friends had known Him in the breaking of the bread, but try as she might she couldn't figure out how this scenario would replay now.

There was nothing for it but to wait and see. Only, the wait was shocking long. A whole week now exactly. Holy Saturday, it was. No one had said anything to her about mass tomorrow—she'd have to find out for herself. Maybe she'd meet a priest there, who could give her some advice. It was three days in the Bible, but then some time after that before the bread thing. Eight days, was it? She had that in the back of her mind. A priest would know, of course.

Eight days? Tomorrow? Here's hoping. The first couple of days in this nasty place hadn't been too bad. She couldn't remember much about them, frankly, because she'd been in a bit of a tizzy after the terrifying business with the knife. She truly hadn't expected anything like that. But, having had a few days now to get her head round what had happened, she'd understood you must expect the unexpected. It was making sense at last. "The Lord moves in mysterious ways," people were always saying. You can say that again, thought Mary-Margaret. Mysterious was an understatement. Flipping puzzling they were, His ways, not to mention frightening.

Fidelma had other visitors in the following week. The first was Alice Armitage, who arrived on Monday with a shopping bag full of vegetables and fruit. She was brisk and sensible and did not linger. Fidelma sensed a reserve in her although she was not unfriendly. On Tuesday it was Mary-Margaret's doctor. He had telephoned the day before to arrange a time. Although Fidelma didn't fully understand who he was and why he was coming, she agreed to see him.

She was surprised when she opened the door to him, having expected someone who looked different. Afterward she wondered at her own surprise. Why should he not be a gentle, weary-looking, middle-aged man in an ordinary jacket, with thin brown fingers and a beard? Fidelma looked at him with interest. His fine bones and the depth of his dark eyes were pleasing. She found she wanted his attention.

But it was Mary-Margaret who interested him, not her. He had a long list of questions. Family history, education, qualifications, childhood illnesses, childhood games, problems dealing with the world. Fidelma, doing her best to answer him, was surprised again, this time by the difficulty of describing Mary-Margaret in words or, indeed, of summoning her early years to mind. Mary-Margaret had been a presence in Fidelma's life since Fidelma herself was not much older than a child. Millstone, thorn in the flesh, peaceable companion, the creature she had kept alive from the beginning—had actually chosen to keep alive and in consequence had no choice later but to carry on so doing. Who now, in a manner of speaking—well, as a matter of fact—kept Fidelma alive in turn. Or used to. Mutually connected, separate and indivisible, of one flesh, of one bone, what else was a child? And, that being so, how could that child be framed in words?

Mary-Margaret had been undemanding, sure, and quiet, and easy to buy off with lollipops and chocolate biscuits. Many a night Fidelma had left her on her own with Cadbury fingers in her reach and orange squash. Until she was maybe five years old Mary-Margaret had slept in a baby's cot, for the bars to hold her safe. Later, when she got so big her feet poked through them, Fidelma had bought a bed for her and a padlock for the door. Locked in, she couldn't come to any harm.

Undemanding yes, and never beautiful. Mary-Margaret had grown from a baby to a plump child, moonfaced, pale-eyed, with straggling hair the greenish yellow color of dry grass and a mouth always a quarter open. No, not beautiful and most unlike her mother. Fidelma stopped to think. So, was she like her father then, this child? Gray-eyed certainly he was, but more than that Fidelma struggled to remember.

Not beautiful, but there was a sweetness to her. And, besides, she *was* a child. While the quiet doctor watched her with his pen poised, Fidelma was stabbed out of the blue by grief. That child, her daughter—had she ever had the things that children need, apart from a roof over her head and chocolate? Providing both of those had been a daily or a nightly battle; by the end of it Fidelma had had no time for the niceties of peace. She had left her daughter to her own devices as a child, and it seemed they got on well enough, the two of them, keeping their own counsel, watching telly after school, side by side and mainly silent. Food there was, no lack of it, most of the time, although not all the time, it must be said.

A memory of Mary-Margaret at the age of about thirteen came suddenly to Fidelma. Fat knees on the old blue sofa, and gray socks, school socks, sagging in sad folds, her head bowed over a plate, full-heaped with spuds and her fork going to and fro, to and fro, from mouth to plate like a thing mechanical. And earlier pictures too: Mary-Meg at three years old standing in her cot and crying. Mary-Meg at a not much older age crouching by her mother's bed and trying to dry her mother's tears with her podgy little fingers. Don't cry, Mammy. It's all right. I'll look after you. Mary-Margaret looking up over and over again with the light of hope shining in her eyes.

When did it go for good, that light? Fidelma wrenched her thoughts back to the doctor. He was asking something about statemented needs and learning difficulties, special provisions made at school. Fidelma couldn't follow. She was afraid she might begin to cry. Something was clenching the muscles of her throat and thistles had grown behind her eyes.

I may have to call again, the doctor said. If that's all right with you. You do understand that it will help your daughter if we collect as much background information as we can?

Fidelma nodded. There's one very important thing, the doctor went on, having looked at Fidelma closely. We may have to go back to it but, if at all possible, I'd like to make a start today. That is the question of Mary-Margaret's religious faith. I've spent quite a lot of time with her in the last few days and what has struck me is the way she talks about religion. So, I wondered if I could ask you: is yours what might be called a religious family? Forgive me for asking. But it may be really crucial to get some facts on that.

A religious family? Fidelma repeated his words to gain some time. For a start, she thought, the answer might depend on what you called a family. Was there such a thing as a family of two? A succession of holy pictures proceeded through her mind—the sort that used to be printed on small rectangles of flimsy card, highly colored and given out as favors by the kinder class of nuns. The Holy Family, Jesus, Mary and Joseph, usually arranged around a lathe or a workbench of a picturesque if not perhaps historical appearance. Well so. There were only three of them. But it must be supposed that Jesus as a little boy was made to say his prayers at night and taken to the temple, whereas Fidelma had not once accompanied Mary-Margaret to church or taught her a single word of any prayer or even said the name of God, except in vain.

No, she told the doctor, firmly. Although I did send her to the nuns. But that was because they ran the only school where Mary-Margaret could go. A smaller size of school, it was. The other school—the closer one—had nigh on a thousand children in it, and Mary-Margaret was frightened. She wet her bed and all, when she first went there—although she had not been in the habit of so doing. The sisters were better for her. For my own part I do not have a lot of time for them and I daresay they did fill her head up with their stories. It could be true to say that Mary-

Margaret is pious. And has been, since a girl. Never misses a Sunday or a feast day if she can, always dipping in and out of church.

Do you usually go with her?

No, Fidelma said again. I have no use for such things now. And, besides, I never leave this flat.

Why is that? the doctor asked.

I am registered disabled, Fidelma said, with dignity and in clear conclusion.

Azin Qureshi stood up. He had observed the suppression of tears and the signs of tension. This poor woman, this monstrously fat woman, was evidently miserable. And with reason. He said good-bye and hoped she would allow another visit. It took a long time for the lift to haul itself up to the nineteenth floor—so long that Azin had begun to think he had better use the stairs.

After the doctor had gone, Fidelma sat down again in her chair by the window. She was very tired. Should she have tried to tell the doctor just how hard it was to rear a child alone, without friends or family to help? To feel yourself an outcast, from your own country, your people, and your church? Well, maybe to rue the last of those was stretching it a bit. When she was a little girl Fidelma went to church on Sundays, right enough. She had liked it, then. She could still remember the excitement of her First Communion, the happiest day of your life it is, the nice old parish priest had said. And he had a point, in general, as far as Fidelma's later life turned out. Yes, she had been happy at the age of seven. Cool sand beneath her feet and meadowsweet, a mammy and a daddy, a fire in the hearth and the voices of the sea. She had worn a veil on her First Communion day. Borrowed it was, from Mrs. McAleevey, who had four grown daughters and was generous to Fidelma's mother. Look at the child, Mrs. McAleevey said when Fidelma showed herself off in the foam of bright white lace, and won't she one day make a lovely bride!

Well, but, that was all before. And later? Would the doctor care to know about the cold rooms of the big house, the bare boards on the floors, the long line of narrow beds, the sound of children quietly weeping through the night like little birds in darkness giving voice to sorrow? Rules and hunger, discipline and punishment; give thanks for what you have, for without the sisters you'd have nothing at all and you'd be on the street to perish.

Was cruelty their pleasure? Fidelma wondered now. And conceded to herself that it was not. Or if it was, only for one or two; the rest were decent enough, it must be said, and a few were positively kind. Looking back, Fidelma saw that they too had suffered hardship, deprivation. Women faced with nothing much—no money and no prospect of a husband, as women are from time to time and always have been—how could they be blamed for taking refuge in a convent? All right, you could accept that some of them had heard the call of God. But not all of them, not the dozens who stood in church in serried ranks, no, that would be beyond belief. For every bride of Christ who sacrificed her life to worship and the care of orphaned children, there must have been another who had nowhere else to go.

In that way, looked at from that angle, the nuns were to be pitied quite as much as the children in their care. More so, maybe, for theirs was a life sentence. And the worst part of it all for them, the want of touch. No nun ever picked a child up, kissed it, held it, felt it soft against her skin. If a child were seen to touch another child, that child would be severely reprimanded. Fidelma was not allowed to kiss her own wee sisters. It was what she minded then and minded still, and missed so much, that longing felt like a great stone weighing down her heart.

Would she have let the doctor see that yearning? Would she tell him how the little girls in the big house in the city cried for their mammies in the night? And what had happened to her when she was caught in the basement kitchen of the house, stealing sugar lumps to comfort one such weeping child? No, she would not, however deep his eyes were and however soft his voice.

She would not tell him because she would not let herself remember. The blackness. The blackness and the choking.

Black ranks of the sisters, black-veiled and white-wimpled, kneeling, heads bowed, in the choir stalls of the church. And the old priest droning: suffer little children. It were better for him if a millstone were hanged about his neck, and he were drowned in the depth of the sea, than that he should cause one of these little ones to stumble.

Take care you do not find yourself alone with him, some of the wee girls whispered of that priest. For he'll put his hand into your knickers while he bids you pray for him. If that were true, Fidelma had no way of knowing. He had not laid a finger on any part of her. But he had remarked to Mother Superior that Fidelma was a bold child who would go to the bad if not taught a lasting lesson. And Mother Superior took those words to heart. Every child in the house over the age of ten had a special duty—polishing the floor, peeling potatoes, folding laundry, and the like.

Only, Fidelma's was the harshest. Scrubbing lavatory bowls by hand each morning, with a can of Vim and a well-worn cloth. Moving from cubicle to cubicle under observation, kneeling on the tiled floor with her face stuck right inside the pan, rubbing at the stains of blood and piss.

They must have shone like finest china, Fidelma thought, like soup tureens from the table of a prince. But however white they gleamed—as ogres' teeth—that nun would not be satisfied. Forever finding fault she was, and Fidelma the butt of all her accusations. Her means of punishment were many. The denial of food at teatime; an hour of being made to stand outside in the courtyard while the rain poured or the snow fell; a beating. And the other one, the worst one, the one that even now Fidelma would not let herself reflect on.

Blackness. The black cloth of priests and nuns was of a curious shade, green-tinged and somehow shiny, like a fly's head, faintly grubby. Fidelma laughed. Black-clad I am myself now, she said to herself, and none too clean at that, I don't suppose. A grimness fell upon her. Even though she was doing her best to fend them off, those memories of the black place crowded in and swarmed and buzzed around her. Here she was, in a room that was as full of light as a glass lantern, but yet she might as well be in the place where they had locked her all those years ago. She was a prisoner now, as she was then, but without any promise of release. There's one way out and one way only, Fidelma thought, with sour amusement at the challenges her coffin would be like to cause in terms of size and weight.

*

Flowers for a funeral? What sort? What would Felix like? Forget-me-nots? Daisies? Probably the kind of flower that grows by waysides and in neglected corners, unregarded, Stella thought. She gave up trying to come to a decision. At least there was a date. And a place, at last. Rufus had wanted the funeral to be held at Felix's school, so that his friends could come to it. Stella knew that Felix would have hated that, but she did not have the strength to argue. Fortunately Barney and Camilla did, and they had overruled their father.

Stella looked at Rufus now, asleep in a chair, with his papers spread across his knees and on the floor around him. Poor Rufus. He was so tired all the time. They all were. Who could have told that death would be so tiring? It was as if grieving were some terrible long-distance race which wrung you out and left you limp and beached. They shoot horses, don't they? Stella thought.

Poor Rufus. Only days after Felix's death, Stella's sister-in-law had told her that bereavement drives couples apart, more often than not, rather than bringing them together. Stella saw that that could happen. For herself, though, she knew that it would not. To part from Rufus would require energy and a depth of feeling Stella would never have again. Even now, when sorrow was as raw as new-flayed flesh, she knew that to be the case. In time a skin would form across her wounds, she knew that too, but it would always be as fragile as a first frost's light glaze on water, and as easy to break through. The hurt beneath would never heal. Nor would she want it to. Forget-me-not.

A state of indifference was what she hoped to reach. A neutral state of being. Neither fevered nor frozen, neither loving nor hating, not wanting, not waiting, expecting no change and caring for nothing, surviving not living, like a primitive creature in the darkest reaches of the sea. You're lucky Felix was not your only, the same sister-in-law had said, in an attempt at consolation. Imagine that! To lose your only child and be too old to bear another. At least you still have Barney and Camilla.

That too was true. And they were the exceptions to her carelessness. She would go on loving them, of course. But, as a whispering snaky voice inside her pointed out, if they were dead, she too could die, which at the moment was the option she desired most. She thought of families she had known who superstitiously refused to travel as a group. Parents flying separately she understood, but not the idea of sharing out the unlikely though potential risk between their children. In spells of turbulence or when the noises in an aircraft suddenly changed key and the knuckles of nervous passengers whitened on their armrests, Stella used to think there would be worse fates than plunging downward through the clouds together.

Worse fates? Well, even now, in the fiercest grip of anguish, Stella knew that her surviving children had their whole lives left to live and would live them well. They would mourn their brother but they would move on and one day they would laugh again and love and perhaps have children of their own. And then they'd learn the deepest form of terror.

Felix had saved her from that terror; she knew that too, already. The thing that every mother dreads most agonizingly had happened and there was nothing left to fear. Felix had conquered death. If a small, defenseless child could die so easily, slipping out of life like a mayfly on a summer evening, breathing at one moment and not breathing the next, then so could all of us. Death was quite disarmed. And, what is more, the knowledge of this death had proved to Stella that those who are left behind can go on living, provided that they live in a state of equilibrium that comes quite close to calm.

And provided that the dead can go on living too, in substance, not as pious metaphor. Felix had lived inside his mother for nine months and now she would carry him again forever. It was not true or right to say the wombs that never bore were blessed. Bearing children had taught Stella the lesson of love, the loss of a child confirmed it. Stella knew the agony she suffered now was equal to the love she felt and that the two were inextricably connected. Without love there could be no sorrow. And who would choose to forgo love so as to spare themselves the agony of loss?

But. There were salt lands, desert places still to cross. The distance between understanding and acceptance was immense. And so conditional, so provisional, so reliant on perhaps, and could, and an imperfect future tense. This was another lesson painfully and slowly learned. That a being as alive and warm and whole as Felix could in the space of seconds be transformed into something that could only be described in the third person and the past. That this child would never *be* again. Stella still could not believe it. If she slept she dreamed that Felix lived, and when she woke, the dawning of the truth hurt so much she cried out loud in pain.

*

This doctor was being seriously stupid, Mary-Margaret thought. How many more times did she have to tell him? Over and over again she had explained. She was a chosen one, a messenger, a dearly loved disciple. But she was the daughter of a sinner. Most people were, it was true to say, sinners, that is; she was one herself. But, unlike her mother, she went to confession regularly and was truly sorry for her grievous faults. Her mother, on the other hand, was in a constant state of mortal sin. So, in order to take away that sin, Mary-Margaret had to make a sacrifice. She knew she had to do it because Jesus had stopped talking to her from the cross. Well, He hadn't exactly *talked* to her in the beginning but He had communicated His great love and she knew He had a special mission for her. When He would not give her a new sign—when He stopped, after the first time, after the veils were taken down—Mary-Margaret had been very upset, and had wondered why He was so angry and what she had done wrong. Then she understood. About the sacrifice. You know. Sometimes it was rams or heifers. Or a pair of doves. But, when it really mattered, it was Isaac. You see, Isaac was someone deeply loved. Abraham, his father, loved him. Isaac was his only son. And of course no one ever loved a heifer like they loved a child. Mary-Margaret understood that she must sacrifice a thing she loved. Which was Shamso. But she also understood that God would not let Shamso die. He had stopped Abraham in the nick of time—just as he was about to plunge his knife into the child—and Mary-Margaret knew that He would stop her too. Which He did. Of course.

Dr. Qureshi could be quite annoying. Yes, all right, he did seem kind and he had lovely eyes but he never let you know what he was thinking. Most people, listening to a friend or hearing the kind of tale Mary-Margaret was growing tired of telling, would widen their eyes or smile or at least look sympathetic. Show that they understood what you were saying. But Dr. Qureshi only nodded. Nod, nod, nod, like a flipping eejit, whatever you did or said. And, when he wasn't nodding, he took notes. Or asked yet another pointless question.

What did you mean by sin? he was asking now. You mentioned that you thought you were the daughter of a sinner?

Well, I used to think she was a widow. My mother, I'm talking about. But, all of a sudden and out of nowhere, she told me she was never married. And that makes me a sinner. In sin did my mother conceive me, and in sin was I born into this world.

Dr. Qureshi nodded. It's not all that unusual, he said. To have children without being married. I'm sure you know lots of single mothers. There's no reason why they cannot love their children and take good care of them.

Mary-Margaret nodded in her turn. She couldn't be bothered to explain. She should have known that Dr. Qureshi wouldn't get her point; he probably didn't know anything about sin, considering where he came from. A shame, it was, in fact. He could be thick but he was such a nice man and she would like to think his immortal soul was safe. She would also like to think he understood about the Morrison child being sent to rescue Shamso, but she was very much afraid that he did not. It was quite complicated, when you thought about it. She wasn't absolutely sure, herself. The eighth day had been and gone. And there was nothing, yet. Was it too hard to get a message to her, in this cold place with its locked doors? No, it wouldn't be that—prison walls and double locks were no barrier to God. Mary-Margaret was beginning to get worried. She needed someone she could turn to, someone who would see the things she saw, unlike this doctor.

She switched her mind to him again. Taking care of children? Loving them? What was he talking about? It wasn't something that had ever crossed her mind. She knew about love, God's love, the deep-down thrilling warmth she felt when she contemplated Jesus; she had felt the same warmth, or something very like it, when she cradled Shamso. Or whenever she set eyes on Father Diamond, in the old days, before he got so shirty and impatient. And, of course, she loved her mother, for she had to, it was what daughters did. It went without saying—just as mothers loved their children; it was a law of nature, like sunset in the evening, or leaf fall, or rivers staying true to the same course. It was the chief commandment. Love.

She stopped thinking for a moment. Into her head came a picture of Fidelma at the door of her bedroom, with a padlock in her hand. Her mother, who was beautiful, until she grew so sad and fat. Did Mary-Margaret ever kiss that creamy cheek and snuggle deep into those arms? She supposed she must have done, but she could not remember. Certainly, when Mary-Margaret got big, she neither gave nor took a kiss; what an odd thing it would be for a grown girl to expect cuddles from her mother! That was for babies, surely, love didn't come into the picture later; not in that way, the way the world took the meaning of the word.

Not everybody knew love was a duty; they got it muddled up with romantic stuff—valentines and flowers.

Hearts and kisses. Mary-Margaret shook her head to get rid of the thoughts that were swarming like flies inside it and making her feel tired and muddled. O sacred heart of Jesus, strengthen me, she said, out loud. And then, more quietly: deep in Thy wounds, Lord, hide and shelter me. She could feel tears prickling her eyes. Could she have got it wrong? Was the little boy an angel? If he were, he'd be immortal anyway, of course, but he wouldn't necessarily come back. Not to see him in the flesh again, not to know he lived? A black thought that, so hopelessly black that it could not be borne. Mary-Margaret, willing it away, began to cry as openly and loudly as a child.

That black thing was crouching on her face. Its foul breath blew rank on her; she was suffocating. Fidelma screamed out loud to make it go, to call for help—and her own voice woke her. She struggled to sit up. It was cruelly dark. Dead of night, she knew it must be, although she could not see to tell the time. She gasped for air. Oh, she had begun to think she would survive. Did she want to? Well, that was another question altogether. One to ask of some part of her other than her mind. And what would that be, that part that lived a separate existence, like a tapeworm in the gut or a microbe in her bloodstream; would you call it the soul? No, the spirit more like, for the soul might equally whisper words of death in the darkness of the night. Was it the spirit that forced a fisherman swept overboard to fight his frantic way up through the tar-black sea to fill his lungs with air again while another voice inside told him: hush now, sink down quietly, you will sleep soundly there, fathoms deep, among the bones of long-drowned men.

Who knows? She had faced dying and she had been reprieved for the time being by packages of food and promises of assistance from various well-meaning bodies. Yesterday evening she had got herself into her nightclothes and her bed, feeling somewhat proud of her achievements. Now this. The black thing come again, to press her down, to fill her eyes and nose and mouth with filthy dust, as if she were a victim of live burial, helpless beneath the weight of earth above her. She had heard of bodies that, exhumed, displayed every sign of having been alive when they were laid in the graveyard six feet under. Mouths agape in horror, fingers turned to claws, their tips worn down to naked bone from scraping vainly at the lids of their own coffins.

She remembered that she had been dreaming in the night of Mary-Margaret dying. Last week the sad-eyed doctor had assured Fidelma that her daughter would be well looked after in the hospital of the mad. We're doing what we can, he said. She has a lawyer. While he was speaking, Fidelma had believed him. But, in the days since, with her partial recovery from shock, Fidelma had been mulling on her daughter's plight. It was said of her that she had killed a child. Fidelma was not ignorant; she knew full well that accusations must be proved in court. Innocent until proven guilty; was that not the phrase? But a child was dead. No lawyer's clever words could bring that child back or assign his killing to another. A child was dead. His name was Felix. And it seemed that Mary-Margaret killed him.

Not for one moment did Fidelma think Mary-Margaret a murderer. She was quite sure that any killing done was accidental. But, try as she might, she could find no explanation for it. Nor excuse. How then would a doctor or a lawyer? Whatever arguments they made, whatever pleas for sympathy, Mary-Margaret would have to pay for killing Felix. And she could only do that by remaining locked away, cloistered from the world, far from any child whom she could hurt, for years and years, if not for the rest of her lifetime.

In the beginning, as the bleak reality of the situation impressed itself upon her, Fidelma was fearful for herself. How could she exist alone here, in her tower-prison, as helpless as a tortoise on its back, as a dolphin washed up on the strand? Later, she began to feel for Mary-Margaret. How would she bear her loss of freedom? A woman yet as childlike as her daughter—what would become of her behind locked doors, in the company of murderers and sinners?

When she was carrying her baby, all that time ago, Fidelma used to worry that the unborn creature would be terrified by the small, dark space in which it found itself. She understood that a child did not miraculously gain consciousness with its first breath. What it knew or sensed or felt in its first minutes on this earth was the same as in the last days before birth. So if a baby cried for fear of darkness in the night when it was put down in its cot, would it not have felt the same fear in the womb? When it grew too big to dance and somersault in its liquid globe, when it could no longer turn, or stretch out a cramped foot, did it not experience sheer panic?

And would Mary-Margaret feel that now in the tight cell of her prison?

Oh God, the tight cell of a prison. Night after night Fidelma was returned in dreams to that black place, the place of punishment. Oh, you willful child, you are so bold and you must be made obedient. Gentle Jesus, meek and mild, take him as your model. In you go and think on him and tell him you are sorry. Only when you're sorry enough will I come to fetch you.

And the shove through the dwarf-size door and the shriek of the rusting bolt jiggled into place. One last vindictive thrust to lock it tight. Dark, dark, dark; so dark it was much safer to close your eyes and keep them closed for the small light there might be behind them. When you opened them, you opened onto darkness that was hot and thick, furry even, as if you were buried by the hide of some great monster. Stone beneath you, the foundations of the building; brick around you, crumbling; the ceiling above you, close above you, arched like a slice of apple, or a rainbow, except there was no light. The vaults of the building these were, old and used for storage, but you as a child believed the bodies of other children rotted in them. Lying on the floor you reached the ceiling with your outstretched hand. You thought, what if the whole place were to tumble down and you in there, a prisoner, buried under a mountain heap of stone? What if Sister forgets that I am here? She is the harshest, her with the sharp nose and the mouth like a hen's vent. And she is forgetful. Where did I put those keys? she'd ask. Whom did I instruct to scrape the porridge from the pot? Why, if she could not remember the words she said but seconds ago, would she not forget that she had shut a child in the cellars? There were other doors to other compartments in these cellars which were always locked. The bones of forgotten children could lie undisturbed in them for centuries as no one in the world would think to wonder that they had gone missing, or to look.

How long would it take to die? Three days and nights, maybe, the time that Lazarus was in his grave—or was that more?—or Jonah in the belly of the whale. You could pretend this dusty tomb that you were in was actually the interior of a fish. That all around you, rather than the heavy weight of brick, was water. Cool seawater, with the sun scattering gold sequins on it and the wind that blows forever ruffling the white lace of the waves.

Three days and nights. But you cannot wait that long. Three minutes are three hours and you know that even if she does come back for you, she will take her time. Something scuttles closer to you. Claws skitter on the stone, sharp teeth chatter, something hisses, there is hot wetness on your leg and you cannot bear this and the terror roils like storm-whipped water in your guts. It's not a feeling, it is real; it rises up through the channels of your blood and fills your head and stops you breathing and you flail around, you are a mad thing, and you scream, but no one hears and no one comes.

Fidelma, drowning in memories and in fear of the future, helpless under the great weight of her flesh, bereft by nightmare of the one small flash of hope that had briefly flickered, sank again into the black pit of her childhood. Now, as then, there was no way out. Then, each time—and in remembrance there were many times—the nun had come back in the end to slide the bolt out of its housing and let the prisoner go. A cobwebbed child, dirt-streaked and damp with fright and piss, sent out into the yard for the smug ones, pets of Sister, who were never caught in mischief, to deride. But now? Who would let her out? Who would understand that it was beyond Fidelma's strength to commit herself again to the coffin of the lift? Not again, not after the long night she had spent in it, with no light, no means of communication, no prospect of rescue. A failure of power supply, she supposed it must have been, when the next day she was free and calm enough to think. But who could say that it would not fail her once again?

She would not, in her waking mind, relive that night if she could help it. The first lurch of the heart when the lights went off and the lift machinery shuddered to a halt. The next minutes of suspense, when she waited for it to start to life again. And then the realization that something was gravely wrong. No light in the panel of buttons, no illuminated means to make the lift door open or to signal alarm. She had her box of matches, and she lit one. By its small flame she depressed the buttons. Methodically at first—doors open—doors open—doors open—and then randomly, in growing panic. Tearing at the door seal with her nails. Banging with her fist. Screaming out for help.

It was about one o'clock on a Wednesday morning. Even in that place of restless souls, nocturnal wanderers, there would not be many who would notice the malfunction of one lift, and fewer who'd do anything about it. Fidelma, again, was trapped, as helpless as a child. She lit a cigarette to soothe her nerves. There were only two left in the packet.

The smell of the man she'd been with was still sticky on her fingers, and the smell of the money he had paid her. Might her smoke swallow all the oxygen there was? Would this metal box admit a breath of air or was it airtight? Would she suck in increasingly shallow lungfuls until she had exhausted the supply? Mary-Margaret would realize she had not come home, but not till halfway through the day. Fidelma, of necessity, kept late hours and often slept till noon. If Mary-Margaret wondered why her mother stayed out at night, she never said so; probably, like all children—although she was by then twenty or so—she did not question what went on around her. In any case, she would not notice Fidelma's absence for some time, she might even go out in the morning, taking one of the other lifts, returning only when it was too late.

Breathing hard and braced for death, marched toward it by the drumming of her heart, Fidelma O'Reilly swam in and out of consciousness for what felt like a lifetime, in the darkness of the broken lift. Repairmen, called by the caretaker, got her out of it at some point in the morning. She must have got into it again, or another one, to reach her dwelling on the nineteenth floor. But whether or not she did, she had no recollection. The terror of the night wiped her memory of the following hours quite clean. It was as if she had been precipitated by it into a numbness that lasted a long time. Only her sense of panic was not obliterated. When she recovered, she vowed absolutely she would never step into a lift again.

Fourteen years ago. And Fidelma had kept that vow. She made it privately; she did not discuss it with her daughter or with anyone else. If there was one thing she had salvaged from her hard life, it was pride. In the yard of the orphanage Fidelma O'Reilly, begrimed and disgraced, had held her head up high.

She couldn't now remember how she had told Mary-Margaret she no longer felt like going out. After a while, her staying at home was just the way things were. Mary-Margaret did the shopping, at which she soon became proficient, and went to the post office to collect their various benefits. Fidelma, trapped now in a tiny space and made desperate by confinement yet even more afraid of the one means of exit, found some comfort in the food her daughter bought. Soft things, sweet things—white bread, chocolate sponge—that cushioned her loneliness and hunger. And her bones also. As if the food were air pumped beneath her skin to make a space around her that was hers, Fidelma ballooned greatly, and as she did, that space became paradoxically heavy, so she could hardly move. Her weight became a medical condition, with the helpful side effect of extra money and certification from the state. Having diagnosed a chronic problem and ascertained that it was manageable, relieved social workers left the O'Reillys to themselves. Disability benefits. Fidelma savagely enjoyed the irony of those words.

She was no one's fool. It had not escaped her that she had made a double prison for herself. Her huge bulk was a cell within a cell, an extra barrier to the outside world. So what? The world outside, nineteen floors below, that world of sour dregs and chip shops, screeching sirens, shit-smeared streets, sad gray drizzle, weary men with forlorn pricks and tightly folded dirty money, had nothing more to offer. She had her drip feed from it in Mary-Margaret.

But now that line was gone. And unlikely to be back. And Mary-Margaret herself in mortal peril.

The blackness of the thing descended on Fidelma like a pall. She jerked violently against it, seized by an overwhelming need to be up and moving, rushing round and throwing windows open, letting in a stream of cold, sweet air. A bat, a bird beating its wings against the walls of a closed room. She flung her coverings off and tried to lever herself onto her side. If she could stretch a little more, the switch on the bedside light would be within her reach. She swung her legs off the side too suddenly; the momentum brought her body with it and she fell, face downward, to the floor, the fall only briefly broken by her knees, which folded instantly beneath her, her whole weight on one buckled arm.

When the time was up, Azin Qureshi showed Mary-Margaret out, her hands still clutching crumpled tissues. He watched her walk away from him, down the corridor, a stumpy figure in shapeless clothes, unsexed and desolate. She swayed a little as she walked, like a drunkard or a toddler. He took a deep breath and exhaled slowly. Her case troubled him. Mary-Margaret O'Reilly's innocence was so transparent, and she so childlike and credulous. Indeed, only a young child could possibly believe the things she said that she believed: messages from Jesus, God in the form of a schoolboy, blood weeping from a statue on a cross. Father Christmas, the Tooth Fairy, nursery tales and myths. On the surface, it was clear that anyone over seven who seriously believed this stuff was mentally unbalanced.

And yet Mary-Margaret, in many ways, seemed reasonably grounded. She showed no symptoms of temporal lobe epilepsy or schizophrenia or any other disorder usually associated with religious mania. In different circumstances he would have said she had nothing more than learning difficulties of a moderate sort. This was, in fact, what other professionals had concluded when she was assessed at school. She was competent enough to take care of herself—she could count and read reasonably well, she could go shopping, cook a basic meal, keep track of money, understand a timetable, catch a bus. In an earlier age she would have been described as slightly simpleminded.

Azin went over to the window and looked down onto the hospital car park, where a constant crawl of drivers searched anxiously for space, and patients, with their minders, went back and forward with bent heads. If he shared Mary-Margaret's cultural background, would he find her easier to understand? Well, but he *did* share it, to all intents and purposes, he who was born in Kensington and went to school at Harrow. All the mornings of his school days he heard chaplains reading prayers and sang the words of Christian hymns. He had played the tunes as well, as an organ scholar at Cambridge. If he had to choose one piece of music to take with him to a desert island, it would be Bach's *St. Matthew Passion.*

This music spun of hope and tears moved him profoundly, as did the fragile ribs of stone that arched above his head in his college chapel, interlaced in pleading, reaching to the sky. But he was equally affected by the adagietto of Mahler's Fifth Symphony—he drew no distinction between the sacred and the secular, for the sacred was meaningless to him. What he saw in those soaring notes and those impossibly perfect traceries of stone was human aspiration. And in this he was like almost everyone else he knew—his wife, his friends, his colleagues. Decent, civilized, tolerant, intelligent; people like him had no use for supernatural solace.

Azin thought of his grandparents, the last generation of his family to live by religious precepts. He could just about remember their rituals of prayer and mosque attendance, the rhythms of a year marked by feast and fasting. His parents had shrugged off these habits; he and his brothers had been brought up to respect their grandparents' traditions as culturally important but no more. He felt the same about Christianity. It was good to be a citizen of a country that kept faith with its traditions; those societies that broke abruptly with the past endangered their own future. He enjoyed the seasonal aspects: Easter, Halloween and Christmas, chocolate eggs and jack-o'-lanterns, a faint ghost of pine scent in the branches of an uprooted Norway spruce—pleasing elements in the rich mix of a culture. Interesting too as symbols: fertility and death, darkness and light, mourning and renewal. Now the green blade riseth from the buried grain . . . the land made waste by the icy breath of winter comes back to life with spring.

It was curious, now that he thought about it, the sliding scale of respect. Primitive rituals score highly—though not perhaps the ones pertaining to sacrifice and blood. But while we are relieved there are no longer Aztecs excavating human hearts, we bow our heads in reverence to the awesome knowledge of the ancients. To build a chamber out of stone so precisely that the sun will find its one small opening at daybreak on the winter solstice every year. Imagine! Hewing the vast stones of the pyramids, the temples at Ajanta, the monoliths on Easter Island, all by hand!

In the West, Azin thought, we calibrate the scale with a compass. The further east, the more respect is paid. Buddhist rituals are especially venerated: prayer flags fluttering in the wind on temples built upon the world's high roof, lotus blossom and irenic monks in saffron robes—there's nothing to dislike. Hindu beliefs are so complex that few Westerners begin to comprehend them, but they admire the power of the symbols: Krishna, lord of life; Kali, the destroyer. Datta. Dayadvham. Damyata. Islamic traditions are more problematic, especially when they relate to women, punishment and law, but it is nevertheless incumbent on us to dignify cultural difference. Christianity, as the compass moves, is a softer target. Harmless at best, a hangover from the past, mildly comic when it comes to vicars and gay bishops, an outrage when it reaches the fundamentalist Midwest. Who could forget the unedifying spectacle of a bellicose U.S. president and a British prime minister joined together in prayer?

But who are the arbiters of what is true and what is not? Azin remembered that desultory conversation late at night in Stella's house. Yes, who decides that the millions who hold the Koran to be the transcribed word of God are sane whereas those who revere the book of Brigham Young are batty and the one who claims to hear voices from above is clinically insane? If it is the case that Aristotle, Plato, Dante, Shakespeare, Beethoven and Bach seriously believed in God, how can we be sure that they were wrong?

And yet mostly we are, thought Azin, returning to his desk. He had to see another patient shortly and to check his notes beforehand; there was no time for theological speculation. We know we are alone here on this earth, without recourse to outside help, and that our short span of life is all there is, he told himself. Or, at least, I know that, speaking for myself. But even so, it is peculiar that we sit round dinner tables, amid the debris of candle stubs and pudding plates, the last drops of Muscat de Beaumes-de-Venise still sticky in our glasses, and we talk of haunted places, eerie feelings, unfamiliar rooms in which we've been startled in the dark. How often have I heard friends mention the cold finger down their spines in the obscure passages of some historic house, or the sense they had of something tragic lingering over places where terrible things were done? In describing these experiences they can only be inferring some survival of the dead. If the spirits of the murdered can still be felt in Auschwitz, are they not, in some way, still with us? And if this form of supernatural presence, why not God?

Why not? Azin asked himself. And spelled out his own answer. It was not within his nature to credit the existence of an omnipotent, eternal being. God was metaphor to him. He cast his mind back to the priest he had interviewed about the O'Reilly case: Alexander Diamond. O'Reilly's parish priest. Evidently an intelligent man; in conversation it transpired he had a degree in maths. Which surely would imply some grasp of logic. The priest had struck Azin as unhappy, isolated possibly, highly strung, but in no way unbalanced. So, did he genuinely believe in a living

God? He had described O'Reilly and his relationship with her most scrupulously, carefully, measuring his words. She could be a bit of a nuisance, he had said. Hanging around like an abandoned puppy, searching for attention, wanting love. There are always women like that, and men too, of course. Priests must be on their guard against them. They can confuse affection meant impartially with something far more personal, they imagine that they have a special understanding with their priest. They seek objects of desire.

Azin had been struck by the words. Objects of desire. He had noted also the priest's conviction that Mary-Margaret was essentially good. Yes, potentially a nuisance, and very slow on the uptake, but reverent at heart, and humble, you could almost call her holy. What she did—or at least what she did before that horrifying thing—she did with love. It was a source of anguish to him that he had not done more to help her. She had been a fixture in the church for years, since she was a child really, attending mass on Sundays and some weekdays, arriving every Thursday morning with a shopping bag full of dusters, waiting humbly for a word of thanks. Part of the furniture, barely noticed, taken for granted it must be said. He reproached himself bitterly. He should have known—but how could he?—what she was incubating. If only he had known. He thought he had persuaded her that what she took to be a vision was only the effect of a bad blow to the head. He remembered saying that when she was still in hospital. She had nodded. He remembered that as well. If only. If only he had taken better care of her, prayed for her, listened to her properly, if only, then Felix would not be dead.

Father Diamond would never know what had been in Mary-Margaret's mind. To the end of his days he would not understand. And to the end of his days he would relive the moment when he saw Felix falling, his blood flowing, and Mary-Margaret O'Reilly screaming with the knife still in her hand.

Azin saw a man in pain. Possibly he'd need some treatment, for post-traumatic stress if nothing else, but it was not Azin's job to say so, or to give it. Although, if he had the leisure, he would like to know Diamond better. An appealing man and an interesting case study. As would be O'Reilly's mother, but again she was no longer his concern. How intriguing though, that enormous woman, with her cool gaze and her hinterland of the unsaid.

Actually, the person he would most like to see again was Stella Morrison, but he had no excuse to do so and could not possibly intrude upon her now. There was nothing she could tell him about Mary-Margaret. But she was in his mind. He kept remembering the evening when he met her and the way her sleeves fell when she raised her arms to push her hair back off her face, her pale wrists. She had served all that food and wine so quietly—so meekly even—without her husband's help. And yet Azin had sensed a strength in her and a rare quality of restraint. He saw how once or twice, when she was about to speak, she changed her mind and spooled her words back to their source, as if they needed more distilling. Or as if she needed to be sure of their reception. He remembered how she had caught his eyes and held them for a moment, and how he had felt, absurdly, that she was reaching out to him. He wanted to believe she was. He wanted a connection. He wanted her to know he understood. But, quite probably, she had barely noticed him. Who was he but another in a chain of strangers, filing through her evenings? Even if he had made an impression on her then, that must surely have been expunged by what she had suffered since. The chambers of her heart must now be filled with tears, leaving no place for him. Azin screwed his eyes tight at the thought of Stella's pain. He felt the stab of it himself, as if they really were connected, separated twins perhaps, or lovers, or entangled quantum particles in lonely miles of space.

Azin closed his file. There was nothing left to add. His conclusion would be that Mary-Margaret O'Reilly was acting while the balance of her mind was disturbed and that she was unlikely to offend again. He would say in evidence that she suffered from delusions. He expected that she would be found guilty of manslaughter but not of murder or intent to murder and would quietly serve her time, under psychiatric care, until she was judged safe to join the outside world again. And afterward? In all likelihood he'd never know what happened to her in the end.

A tentative knock on the door signaled the arrival of his next appointment. Why, at the end of this case, did Azin feel dissatisfied and sad? He didn't have time to answer but he did make a note to telephone Father Diamond. The priest would surely know about the funeral arrangements. Azin suddenly felt an urgent need to be there, to be part of it, as Stella's friend.

*

Father Diamond and Father O'Connor found Fidelma on Saturday afternoon. By then she had been lying helpless on the floor, with a broken arm, for forty hours. She was confused, dehydrated and she stank of urine; it took a long time before she came to her senses, recognized them and could tell them what had happened.

Father O'Connor had only come home from San Antonio, Texas, via New York and Dublin, the day before. Shocked by the news of Felix's death, he was also very angry. You should have told me, he said to Father Diamond. This happened two weeks ago. You told me about the nonsense with the cross. So why not this?

I didn't think, Father Diamond said. You were so far away. I'm sorry. But what could you have done?

I could have prayed, the older man told him.

He was home in time for Alice Armitage's party. Alice fussed over her hero son like a stable lad attending to a thoroughbred fresh from a great win. She kept her eyes fixed on him as if in one moment's inattention he might vanish, and she patted him each time she passed. There were plates of food on every flat surface in the room—food enough to feed a regiment, food to weigh Fraser down and tie him to home ground. Food to tell her son the things she could not say in words: that she loved him, that a beat of her own heart was missing all the time that he was gone, that she knew she might have had to cook for a funeral instead of a homecoming.

Flooded with relief, glad also that Father O'Connor had come back, Alice was nevertheless in great distress. Finding a quiet moment on her own with Father O'Connor, she told him why. It's like God would only keep one boy alive, she said. I was praying for Fraser at the very moment that the knife went into Stella's son. I was praying: keep my son safe. I feel it was an exchange. And Stella lost. And it's so unfair. I've got Fraser back, not a hair on his head harmed; God gave me that. But Stella's son is dead. And he was only a little thing, his life had just begun.

Father O'Connor saw her reddened eyes. He drew her to him. It doesn't work like that, he said. That much I know. Lives are not held in balance, we don't make bargains with Our Lord. Even if we wanted to, we couldn't. He didn't take her son instead of yours. The young boy died, and that's a terrible thing, but not because you prayed for Fraser.

Then why? she asked.

Oh Alice, Father O'Connor said. If I knew that, I'd be a holy saint for sure, and not a bumbling old fellow all too aware of his shortcomings. That cry—your cry—goes up to heaven every single second of each day. And has done since the dawn of time, and will do until doomsday. Why? If Fraser had been killed out there—and the Lord be thanked that he was not—you would have cried the same. As Stella Morrison is doing now. And I don't know the answer. If there is one, it's an answer that God whispers very softly into hearts that grieve, and I do fear it often goes unheard and takes its time in coming.

So it's not much of an answer, is it, when all's said and done?

No, Father O'Connor agreed. But I believe that those who seek it, and who listen, may find that it's consoling, given time. So, Alice, you were there, I hear, when the child died?

I came too late, she said. He died in hospital, but the knife went deep and by the time I reached him I think he was already going.

I cannot think that Mary-Margaret O'Reilly meant to murder, Father O'Connor said. I always felt she was a *duine le Dia,* a fool perhaps, but a fool of God.

Later on that evening the priest called to mind Fidelma. How's the old dote doing? he asked Alice. She told him she'd delivered food to her on Monday but had not seen her since. I'll go round tomorrow, he said.

Father Diamond drove him there. When there was no immediate answer to their knock on Fidelma's door, he presumed she was going to be as slow to open it as she had been the time before. The two men went on knocking and calling through the letter box but still got no response. Perhaps she's out? Father Diamond suggested.

No. She never goes out. Or, at least, she never has, in all the years I've known her.

Why?

I don't know. She's a recluse. I'd like to think she's a holy anchorite, but the truth may be she's just plain lazy. Or embarrassed.

It can't be good for her. For her health.

Well, clearly it is not. You've seen the woman.

So, should we leave it and come back another time?

No, said Father O'Connor. I've an uneasy feeling.

So they trooped back down to the ground floor and Father Diamond again began the long process of locating the caretaker. This is a godforsaken place, Father O'Connor remarked while they were waiting for him to find a key. He looked at the stained concrete and the rubbish blowing like tumbleweed round the feet of the tower block. But the views are great when you reach the top, he added.

The front door yielded to the key; Fidelma had neglected to put the chain on when she went to bed. At first they thought the flat was empty. The air was still and heavy, stale with smoke. A mug with dregs of tea stood on the table by the window. Mrs. O'Reilly, Father O'Connor called. The door to one of the rooms off the small corridor was open and the other closed. They looked round the open door and saw the bedroom of a child, soft toys piled on the single bed, posters of baby animals on the walls. The bed had not been made. Father O'Connor knocked on the other door and heard a moan in answer.

Fidelma had tried to drag herself across the floor away from the bed, making for the door perhaps, but had stopped before she reached it. She was still lying on her front. At the sound of the door opening, she painfully raised her head. Don't come anywhere near me, she said.

Mrs. O'Reilly, my old friend, Father O'Connor said, entering the room. Fidelma. The curtains were drawn and it was difficult to make things out in the half dark. There now, Fidelma. You've taken a bit of a tumble by the look of things, he said. Ignoring her mumbled protests, he crouched down beside her and stroked her hair off her forehead. Her eyes were not quite focused.

Is it angels that you are? she said. Or answers? The last rites? Or am I already dead?

Father Diamond crouched down too. He didn't think she recognized him. Hello, Fidelma, he said softly. It's me. Alexander Diamond. And Father O'Connor back from America to visit you. Will we get you to your feet?

The two men pushed and pulled, but ineffectually. They couldn't tell how badly she was hurt and dared not risk more damage. Father Diamond rang for an ambulance. He could hardly speak. This woman lying like a fallen tree, a stranded creature from the sea, magnificent, immobilized, her stained nightgown crumpled underneath her, monumental thighs red-streaked with a tracery so delicate, the thinnest rivulets of blood rising to the surface of her skin, expressed the whole world's suffering to him just at that moment. An idol brought to earth, weeping, stinking, unloved, humiliated and alone, trying to pull her clothing down. When she opened her mouth, he saw that she was toothless.

No ambulance, she whispered. Must stay here. No lift.

Father O'Connor leaned in closer. What's that you're saying? he asked.

Can't be going anywhere, no lift.

Father Diamond understood. Although he could not have known what had happened to Fidelma in the past, he saw now with complete clarity, as if through different eyes that were not his own. He saw her trapped in darkness, unable to escape. I'll stay with you, he said. You'll not be on your own in it, I promise. She said nothing then, but closed her eyes. Tears spilled through the fret of her eyelashes.

In the event it was not a simple matter to get Fidelma to the ambulance. Buzzing round like tugboats sent to rescue a wrecked liner, the paramedics finally managed to hoist her to her feet. Although she was unsteady, they decided in the end she had to walk out of her flat and to the lift. A stretcher was obviously impracticable and she did not fit into the wheelchair they had with them. Luckily, the only thing she'd broken was her arm. In the bathroom, Father Diamond found her teeth. Fidelma endured the manhandling in silence. Her one protest was when they reached the lift and the paramedics told the priests they were no longer needed. Then she refused to move without them. Somehow they all squeezed into the tiny space and Father Diamond held her hand the whole way down.

After the ambulance had gone, the priests went back to the flat to straighten it out and lock it up. Father Diamond opened the window in the sitting room, and the wind blew in. He looked out at the city spread before him. The distant hills. She would have died, he said to Father O'Connor in the room behind him, without turning round. If not for you. I wouldn't have thought of going to see her this weekend. I'd have put off visiting until next week, if I'd gone at all.

Father O'Connor smiled at the hunched shape of the younger man, his figure dark against the brightness of the glass. For one fleeting moment he was looking at a saint. Then Father Diamond turned, and Father O'Connor saw the expression in his eyes. What a failure I am, he said.

I'll disagree with you, said Father O'Connor. That's not true, as a matter of fact. I saw the way she held your hand. And you may not think it now—how could you?—but you'll be better for all this, you know. But would you get a move on in the meantime? I'm on for mass in twenty minutes.

Lily of the valley, wood anemones and primroses, on a coffin so ridiculously small. How could anything so small contain the future that was the child who had lived? Father

Diamond aspersed Holy Water on it, tears or drops of dew. The funeral of a child is a funeral of hope, Father Diamond thought. He cometh up and is cut down like a flower, a woodland flower in a world of dew. He fleeth as it were a shadow, and never continueth in one stay.

Stella, in the front row, was as thin as glass. Women in the final stage of pregnancy hold themselves with care, as if they were chalices brimful of liquid. Stella held herself as carefully because otherwise she'd splinter into pieces, not because she carried something precious. She was scoured out and hollow.

Rufus held her hand. Barnaby and Camilla were beside her, and the church was full. Father Diamond processed slowly from the coffin to the altar, behind a boy from the parish bearing a lighted candle. He faced the congregation. Alice and Larry Armitage were there, with Mr. Kalinowski. Dr. Qureshi at the back. And, also at the back, Fidelma, one arm in plaster, white against her draperies of black. Father Diamond already knew that she was coming. She had asked him if she could. Discharged from hospital, temporarily housed in sheltered accommodation, with the promise of her own place at ground level, Fidelma had a chance. If she could, she would have exchanged it for the life of Stella's son.

Will the mother mind that I am there? she'd asked.

I think she'd be pleased, Father Diamond said. Although I can't be sure.

She'll have no need to speak to me, Fidelma said. But, if you tell me that I may, I'll be there to grieve. For her child and for mine. I want to do that in the rightful place; a place where prayers are heard.

Father Diamond nodded but said nothing. Fidelma was no believer, he'd been told, but he had no intention of interrogating her.

Lord of all kindliness, the congregation sang. Lord of all grace. Tears in their voices, some of them. Some already weeping, dabbing at their eyes and widening them, sucking in their cheeks to stem the flow. Many of the women wore bright colors—children's colors—red and green and yellow. Not Stella. Stella was altogether in black, although bareheaded; golden hair like treasure carelessly discarded; she'd have torn it in fistfuls from her scalp if custom had allowed. She'd cover herself in ashes if she could.

Our mourning is so decorous, she thought. Floral tributes in the form of angels, cards of sympathy. My friends, the mothers of living children, shunning inappropriate black. And shunning me, as if I brought contagion. As if my son might take their children by the hand and lead them to their deaths. Finding it hard to speak to me, they say to one another: I can't imagine what she's going through.

And that's true. They can't imagine. But there's enough charity left in me to hope they never will. Meanwhile I'll wear my sackcloth, and my mourning will cry to heaven.

She stood very still, and upright. Pale as candle wax. Be there at our sleeping, and give us, we pray, your peace in our hearts, Lord, at the end of the day.

The funeral rites are the same rites whether the dead be nonagenarian or child. Eternal rest give unto him, O Lord, and let perpetual light shine on him. Priest and people moved through the ceremony along the ordained path, kneeling, standing, following the words that were strange to a few, familiar to most, consoling to them all, if only because they were well-used. Barnaby read from an essay Felix had written about silver eels on their mysterious journey back to the Sargasso Sea where they were spawned. Rufus paid tribute to his son with love and tears. Camilla read from the Gospel of St. John: "At that time, Martha said to Jesus: Lord, if thou hadst been here, my brother had not died, but now also I know that whatsoever thou wilt ask of God, God will give it thee. Jesus saith to her, Thy brother shall rise again."

This is a child who was wholly innocent and wholly loved, Father Diamond said. Weeping at his grave, we make our song.

When the funeral mass was ended, he made the sign of the cross and blessed the congregation.

To us who are alive
May He grant forgiveness
And to all who have died
A place of light and peace.

Two of the undertaker's men lifted the coffin, which one of them could easily have carried on his own. Father O'Connor would go with the family to the graveside. Father Diamond would join them later at their house, where they were inviting friends to celebrate Felix's life. He waited as they filed from the church. Stella had stayed dry-eyed. God grant her the gift of tears, he prayed. And give her the dew of heaven. She walked passed Fidelma, not knowing who she was. Fidelma kept her head bowed and was one of the last to leave. Father Diamond watched her go, supporting herself on crutches, moving very slowly but moving nonetheless.

An empty church; the candles on the altar all extinguished, the vessels and the vestments put away, the sacristy doors locked and Alexander Diamond lying facedown on the tiled floor of the Chapel of the Holy Souls. He was so drained, so tired he felt he'd never have the strength to get back on his feet. He would have liked to close his eyes and stay there while the dust settled slowly on him and his bones crumbled until they mixed as one substance and he was nothing that a light wind could not easily blow away.

It was the final day of April, five weeks to the day since Mary-Margaret O'Reilly had tumbled to this same floor off the altar and in her addlement set out upon a way that led to a child's death. A way on which other souls had been distracted and no one could say they stumbled on a truth. A way he should have barred, like the Archangel with his flaming sword, to protect those souls who were entrusted to his care. That he had not—that he had been too busy gazing at his own soul to see into the souls of others— weighed him down as heavily as the heaviest wooden cross. Lord, I am not worthy, Father Diamond prayed. Lamb of God, have mercy on my soul. Lord, I am not worthy to receive you, but only say the word.

The floor was cold beneath him, the clay hard against his face. His fear was great; of nothing but an infinity of empty space, of endless miles of blackness broken only by the light of dead stars reaching down to earth to drown in its implacable, indifferent seas. Is it madness then? he asked. Am I as mad as Mary-Margaret and the girls who swore that your eyes moved and your wounds bled? All of us, deluded fools, butts of some great cosmic joke, whistling in the dark?

He raised his head to look up at the figure on the crucifix above him. It was silent and unmoving. He let his head fall back again, stopping his mouth against the floor, breathing ingrained coldness and years of hopeful footsteps.

He lay like that a long time—he did not know how long—with his eyes closed and his mind aching, and while he was there, he thought of something, words he'd known or, perhaps, not known at all but heard now for the first time in a voice that was as strange and as familiar as a father's to the newly born. Listen, said the voice, for these words are faithful, and true. Behold, I have refined you, but not as silver. I have chosen you in the furnace of affliction. I form the light, and create darkness; I make peace, and create evil. I am the Lord, and I do all these things. I am the light, and I make all things new.